MISTLETOE AND MISTAKES

KIRSTEN S. BLACKETER

DEDICATION

Readers. This one is for you. Enjoy. xoxo.

My trope-a-thon holiday novella is finally in print!

Hey 2020, Fuck You.

Embrace the suck.

A Letter from the Author

Dear Reader,

We all love tropes (and microtropes.) So here is a sweet and spicy holiday treat brimming with as many as I could fit into a novella without seeming gratuitous.

As a Pennsylvania girl at heart, I couldn't have picked a better setting for a snowed in, matchmaking grandma meddling, best friend's brother, holiday romance.

Enjoy!

With best wishes and love,

Kirsten S. Blacketer

P.S. I used Sebastian Stan as inspiration for Andrew, if you really wanted to know. *wink*

TABLE OF CONTENTS

Chapter One   1

Chapter Two   6

Chapter Three   10

Chapter Four   15

Chapter Five   19

Chapter Six   23

Chapter Seven   28

Chapter Eight   32

Chapter Nine   36

Chapter Ten   41

Chapter Eleven   45

Chapter Twelve   50

Chapter Thirteen   56

Chapter Fourteen   62

Teaser *A Lockdown Love Affair*   69

Teaser *A Holiday Love Affair*   76

About the Author   85

CHAPTER ONE

ANDREW

When I pull into the driveway, I cringe at the obscene amount of Christmas decorations littering my Grandmother's porch. How the hell was an eighty-year-old woman nimble enough to string all those lights and garland herself? The small cabin bears a strong resemblance to those rustic homes adorning the holiday cover of *Good Housekeeping* or *Farm Life*. I shake my head and groan. I hate Christmas.

I turn off the car and groan, pinching the bridge of my nose. Deep breath in. Deep breath out. Of all the years for Grams to beg me to come home, she chose the year from hell. Between the pandemic and the mess at Solus, this year should be cancelled completely. But when Grandma Ruth requests your presence, that's the equivalent of God handing down a commandment. It's strange it took her this long to ask.

The cold air bites my face and fingertips when I step out of the car's warm haven. I grab the decorative paper bag sitting on the front seat and make a mental note to get my duffle from the trunk later.

"Andy, is that you?"

I spin around to find Grams waving from the front porch wearing a hideously festive apron. My gaze narrows. Is that...the Mandalorian on her apron? I almost laugh at the absurdity of seeing my grandmother wearing *Star Wars* anything, but I sober quickly when I remember she's the one who introduced me to the original movies when I was a kid.

"Hey, Grams. Nice apron." I wrap her in a warm hug and hold tight. The sweet, spicy bite of cinnamon and cloves lures me deeper into her embrace. She's so soft and petite in my arms. I cling tighter knowing I've been remiss in visiting her. It's been way too long.

Grams pulls away and her warm, knowing gaze skims across my face and down over my torso. "Look at you. Not the scrawny boy who rode dirt bikes past the sheriff's house at midnight anymore are you?" I catch a glimpse of tears shining behind her glasses as she tuts and turns away. "Come inside before your catch your death."

I shake my head. "I wouldn't put it past fate after the year we've had," I mutter under my breath as I follow her into the house.

The inside of her home looks as grotesquely over decorated as the outside. The small living room bears the marks of Grams' overenthusiastic decorating. An overburdened tree stands sentinel in the corner of the room, years of Christmas ornaments hanging from the branches. Candles and glittering garland interwoven with holly clutter the mantel over the fireplace. A row of stockings hangs from hooks. I see a handmade stocking emblazoned with my name on the end.

"Did you decorate the house by yourself?" I weave through the living room following her into the kitchen.

"I did." She glances up from the open oven with a tray of fresh cookies in her hand. "Do you like it?"

Guilt grips me with meaty fists at the thought of lying to my grandmother, but I smile. "Yeah, it looks good."

She waves her hand. "You're full of it. I saw the look of horror on your face when you got out of the car." She sets the cookies on the stovetop and closes the oven before turning it off. "Never did get into the Christmas spirit, did you?"

I lean against the door frame and fold my arms across my chest. "Nothing gets by you, does it, Grams?"

"Never has, never will." She winks.

Every surface in the kitchen is covered with cookies. Tupperware and tins stacked five high, full of delicious baked goods.

"Are you expecting to feed an army?" I gesture to the

cookie hoard.

Grams laughs. "Not an army. Just the whole town. I'm taking them to the community center. They're having a party tonight for the whole town." She cocks her head and a silver curl escapes the bun holding the unruly curls. "Didn't I tell you?"

Frustration sets in. I came to visit my grandmother, not the whole fricking town. "No, Grams, you forgot to mention that."

She unties her apron and pulls it off revealing an ugly Christmas sweater bearing the face of The Child. "You don't mind giving me a hand getting these into town, do you?"

"No, Grams." I inhale sharply, resigned to the holiday torture I actively avoid. Seems only fitting as the crowning jewel to the year from hell.

"Load these up and we'll head into town."

What felt like twenty trips to my car later, every box, tub, and tin of cookies in the house is loaded in the trunk and overflowing into the backseat of my car.

"Grams! Are you ready to go?"

Grams appears from the bedroom down the hall with a glittering box in her hands. She thrusts it into my chest. "Here. Open it."

I roll my eyes and take the box jammed into my ribcage. "Thanks."

Inside the box is a sweater. I pull it out, bracing myself for some corny ugly Christmas sweater. Then I see what's on it and grin.

"Kylo Ren?" I laugh and hold it up to get a better look.

"Of course." Grams tosses the box aside and turns the sweater to hold it up to my chest. "I had to guess on the size, but I think I did well considering I haven't seen you in years."

"Did you make this?" I ask, eyeing her with newfound respect and a twinge of guilt at the truth in her observation.

"No. Martha down at the center made it." She pulls at her own sweater. "I had her make this one for me."

"'This is the way,'" I mutter in a reverent tone.

"'I have spoken,'" she replies in an equally reverent tone.

"I love it. Thank you, Grams." I pull her into a hug.

She sniffs and wipes a stray tear from her cheek. "Good. Now put it on. We need to get into town."

"Wait. You want me to wear this tonight?"

"Well, of course. Why else would I give it to you before Christmas?" She tuts. "Go, hurry. We need to help set up."

After I change into the warm sweater, we leave for town. Grams flips through the radio stations until she finds the local station playing Christmas music. I grit my teeth, but grant her this small concession. It's only a fifteen-minute drive to the center. So, I bear the torture as we weave down the mountain with Grams singing along with the music.

By the time we reach our destination, my ears are bleeding and my head aches. All I want is a hot toddy and some time to myself. Unfortunately, I'm stuck with the whole town of Coppany and the misery that is the Christmas holiday.

Between songs, a weather alert comes on. "Snowstorm coming from the Great Lakes sweeping over northern Pennsylvania threatens at least a foot of snow. Possible freezing rain starting at midnight."

"You sure about this party tonight?" I glance at Grams. "Sounds like a hell of a storm coming in. Maybe we should stay home."

Grams waves her hand in dismissal. "Since when can weathermen predict the weather? We'll be fine."

We pull into the lot, and it's already packed with cars and people milling around the building. It looks as festive as Grams' house, and I wish I thought to pack my flask. It's going to be a long evening.

My gaze drifts to the store bedside the center. An oversized tree blinks with bright lights and the sign above the store is trimmed in green, silver, and red garland. Buck Wild Beans.

"When did they put that in?" I ask Grams as we climb out of the car.

"Oh, almost ten years now." Grams waves to a group of her friends gathered near the door of the center. "We go there twice a week for book club and bunco. They host all kinds of events in town. Good coffee too." She smiles and turns to the older woman as she walks up. "Julia! So lovely to see you. Would you mind getting some help to carry these cookies in?"

"Right away, Ms. Ruth." Julia rounds up a few people and I step aside as they swarm my car.

"Would you get me a cappuccino, dear?" Grams appears by my side and I jump at her question.

"Uh, yeah. Sure." I leave Grams and the cookies in Julia's capable hands and wander toward the front door of Buck Wild Beans. The logo of a buck drinking a cup of coffee makes me chuckle.

The bells above the door jingle when I open the front door. A familiar and intoxicating scent of coffee beans and fresh baked pastries lures me deeper into the shop. I admire the simple wood décor even though it looks like Santa's elves vomited all over it. The soft strains of holiday music filter through the speakers and I ignore the persistent earworms trying to burrow into my head.

A dark haired woman appears behind the counter from the kitchen.

"Welcome to Buck Wild Beans! What can I get for you..." Her voice trails off when our eyes meet. Those lovely green eyes I spent years trying to forget widen in surprise before narrowing with unabashed suspicion.

"Vivian." A name I haven't spoken in twenty years ghosts over my tongue without a thought.

"Andrew." Her chipper tone dissipates instantly, replaced with icy indifference. "What the hell are you doing here?"

It seems twenty years wasn't long enough. "Grams wants a cappuccino."

Without a word, Vivian turns to the espresso machine. I watch her work and my heart twists in my chest. I anticipated encountering a few ghosts from my past, but I wasn't prepared for the jolt of regret and guilt driving knives into my heart at the sight of my sister's best friend. The one I ruined and left behind without a second thought.

Shit. Could this holiday get any worse?

CHAPTER TWO

VIVIAN

The noise from the machine blocks the world around me. I busy my hands making the cappuccino to keep from throwing a coffee mug at Andrew's head. Fury bubbles in the pit of my stomach as I steam the milk.

Andrew freaking Cooper. Of all the people in the world, why did he have to walk through my doors? I pour the espresso into the milk and push the unprofessional, murderous thoughts from my mind.

I try not to take my anger out on the cappuccino. Grandma Ruth is one of my best customers. She comes to the shop multiple times a week and always brings her groups here for their meetings. It's not her fault her grandson is the biggest asshole on the eastern seaboard.

With as much grace as I can muster, I snap the lid onto the coffee cup and set it on the counter. "Anything else?" I glare at the man who ruined my life.

"No." He pulls his wallet out as I ring up the sale.

My gaze drifts over him out of the corner of my eye. Shit. He's more handsome than he was in high school, even with that ridiculous ugly sweater. *Is that Kylo Ren?* I roll my eyes. He always was a nerd with a soft spot for those ridiculous science fiction shows. His bedroom was littered with posters and his bed...nope, not going there. I shake my head.

"Three fifty." I hold out my hand.

He places a five in my palm, his fingertips brushing mine as he pulls away. I jerk my hand back and retrieve his change. When I offer it, he shakes his head.

"Put it in the tip jar." He offers a half smile. "Good to see you, Viv."

The nickname triggers memories I wish I could have purged and burned long ago. I nod and retreat into the kitchen until I hear the bells over the door signal his departure.

When I poke my head around the corner, the shop is deserted. I sigh in relief, but my heart longs for another glimpse of Andrew.

"No, you're not going to start that shit again." If I say the words aloud, maybe they'll sink in and take root. I cross the room and flip the open sign to closed. Once the door is locked, I lean against it. Why did I volunteer to help at the winter festival tonight?

After I clean the shop and put everything away for the night, I slip out the back door and cross to the rear entrance of the community center. Molly and Debbie are unloading the last of the supplies from their catering van.

"Need a hand?" My breath creates a frosted plume in the evening air.

"Nope. We're all finished unloading, but if you want to head inside, Ruth was looking for you." Molly gestures toward the main room used for gatherings.

"Thanks." I slip inside and weave through the kitchen greeting everyone as they work. My phone vibrates and I pull it out to see a weather alert issued for Warren, McKean, and Potter counties. Heavy snow and freezing rain starting at midnight.

"Something wrong, honey?"

I glance up to find Ruth staring at me over her reading glasses. "No. It's a weather alert for later tonight. We should make sure everything is wrapped up before midnight to be sure no one gets caught in the storm."

"Was it snowing yet?"

"Not yet."

Ruth grins. "Then don't worry. Let's enjoy the festivities."

I tuck my phone in my pocket and nod. "You're right. We've worked hard to get this together. It would be a shame to cancel it over nothing."

"Exactly." Ruth adds with a sage nod. "Would you mind

giving Andrew a hand? He's over at the hot chocolate table."

My teeth clench for a moment before I respond. "Sure."

Ruth pats my arm and ambles off toward the cookie table.

I take a deep breath. "God, grant me the serenity not to murder Ruth's grandson."

Andrew's back is turned when I approach the table. He's carefully measuring out hot chocolate into cups.

"Why are you here?" I can't help but let the snark seep into my tone.

Andrew straightens slowly before turning. "My grandmother insisted."

"How sweet of you." I scoff.

His dark eyes fix on mine. "I can think of much more enjoyable activities than this."

My heart flutters at his words and the intensity of his gaze. Heat creeps into my cheeks at the implication of his words and the smart-ass response melts on my tongue.

"Like a root canal." He smirks and turns back to the hot chocolate.

Shame at my body's reaction and my brain's ridiculous interpretation of his words causes the frustration coursing through me to overwhelm my common sense. "If you hate Christmas so much, then leave. No one will miss you." I fold my arms across my chest. "I'll make sure Ruth makes it home safely."

Andrew sets the cup in his hand aside and faces me. A shadowed challenge reflects in his eyes and I remember exactly why I fell for him so long ago. His ability to take control of a situation should be terrifying. Should be. Operative words. All I want is for him to end my suffering and leave, for good this time.

"Oh, good. I'm glad to see you two have reconnected. You were friends in high school, weren't you?" Ruth magically appears beside her grandson.

I didn't have the heart to correct her assumption. We went to high school together, but Andrew was three years ahead of me and my best friend's brother. And I had a crush on him for longer than I care to admit. At least until he made it perfectly clear how little he cared for my company.

"Andrew, would you mind running home to get my medication? I left it beside my bed." Ruth gestures to me. "Vivian can tag along with you so you both can catch up."

"Sure, Grams." Andrew's response seems innocuous enough on the surface, but the tension between us reverberates through my entire body.

Shit. I could back out, but I never was one to turn down a challenge. Hell, that's part of why we're stuck in this ridiculous predicament now. I smile at Ruth.

"We'll be back in a flash, Ruth. Anything else you need?"

"Just my medication, thank you, dear." She pats my cheek tenderly and leaves us to fume silently at each other once more.

Andrew stalks toward the door and I follow behind him.

Darkness settled fully outside, and the streetlights glow in the haze. A storm is coming. I can taste it on the winter air, but I'm afraid it's going to be much worse than a little snow and freezing rain.

Once I'm buckled in the front seat of Andrew's car and we're heading out of town, sleet pelts the windshield.

CHAPTER THREE

ANDREW

I grip the steering wheel tighter and slow my speed as I turn the car onto the mountain road leading to Grams' house. Should I turn around and get Grams to take her home before the roads get worse? Not that it matters at this point. I'm already halfway to her house and there's nowhere to turn around on this road.

The roads are slick with ice and white flakes fall faster the closer we get. I glance at Vivian out of the corner of my eye. Her grip on the door handle tightens with every passing moment.

"Watch the road." She shoots me a sidelong glare and slides her left hand over her thigh in a repetitive soothing motion.

Even though I've been gone for twenty years, I know these curves like the back of my hand. But she's right. I should focus on the road. The car skids a bit as we take the final corner before Grams' driveway. The backend slides over the icy road and fishtails, but I recover quickly, narrowly missing the ditch, and turn into the driveway.

The gravel helps keep the car on the driveway, but the snowfall steadily increases. By the time we reach the house, I can barely make out the shape of the cabin behind a flowing curtain of white flakes.

"Wait here." I leave Vivian in the car and dash into the house. Inside, I find the pills on the nightstand next to Grams' bed, right beside the picture of Grandpa. The glow of the Christmas lights leads me back through the house to the front door.

When I climb back into the car, I'm coated in fluffy white flakes. Vivian glances up from her phone and stifles a smile before turning away.

"We should get back." I start the car.

"Yeah," she mutters under her breath. "Looks like the storm hit early."

Snow encases the car blurring the cabin and the trees. Shit. We need to get back to town. I should've brought Grams home when I had a chance. There's no way in hell my car will make the trek through the snow if it keeps coming down at this rate.

I'm about to put the car in drive when my phone rings. I answer it when I see Gram's face appear on the screen.

"Did you make it okay?" Grams' asks without missing a beat. "Is it snowing at home?"

"Yeah. It's coming down pretty heavy up here." I glance out the windows and cringe. "I have your pills. We're heading back now before the roads get too bad."

"Don't come back here to rescue me. I'm fine. We cancelled the festival once the sleet started. Julia's letting me stay with her until the storm passes."

"What about your pills?" I ask, gritting my teeth against the response I know is coming.

"Oh, I found some in the bottom of my bag." She chuckles. "I'll be fine. Stay where you are. I don't want you driving in this weather."

"Grams." I fight to keep the exasperation from my tone. "You're lucky I love you."

"I love you too, Andy." She blows kisses through the microphone. "Now, get inside and make Vivian some hot cocoa. There's some goulash in the fridge you can warm up for supper." She hangs up before I can respond.

I stare out the front windshield and contemplate the situation I've found myself in. My grandmother is the smartest, most resourceful woman I know, and I'm clever enough know a set up when I see one. With a heavy exhale, I turn off the car.

"Come on." I step out of the car.

"Wait!" Vivian shouts as the door closes. In the next breath, she's stomping up the snowy path behind me. "We aren't going back to town?"

"Not until the roads clear." I can't even see the driveway

through the trees any longer.

"No. You need to get me back to town. I'm not staying here alone with you." Snowflakes pepper Vivian's dark hair. A few settle on her eyelashes.

While the situation is not ideal, I can't completely share her disgust at being snowed in together. She may not like me. Okay, she may hate my guts, but the idea of getting a chance to spend some time alone with Vivian Holloway has my stomach twisted in knots and my heart racing.

We face off, snow and tension swirling between us. "Look. The roads are shit. My car won't make it down the mountain. Grams is safe with Julia, so there's no reason to risk our necks."

"The pills?" Her voice softens a smidge, but indignation burns hot in her eyes.

"False alarm. She found them in the bottom of her purse." I purposely avoid bringing attention to the fact that Grams completely set this whole thing up. I wouldn't put it past her to be in cahoots with God in order to move up the snowstorm's timetable. But honestly, I'm going to blame the weatherman for being incompetent.

"Oh." Vivian draws her lip between her teeth and shivers. Part of me wants to reach out and pull her against me. To show her exactly how much I regret what happened in high school. Damn it. I could almost forget any time has passed and we're right back where it all started. There was a huge snowstorm that night too.

"Come on. Grams said she's got some goulash in the fridge and I'm starving." Without another thought, I turn and head inside.

Vivian follows behind and shakes off the snow before stepping inside the house. She slips off her coat and scarf, hanging them up on the hook behind the door. I do the same and head into the kitchen. The drive to keep my hands busy also keeps my mind occupied.

I start the stove and put the goulash in a pot to simmer while putting the kettle on another burner. The scrape of the chair on the linoleum echoes behind me. Ignoring the pull of her presence, I reach into the cabinet and retrieve two bowls and two large coffee mugs.

"Do you know what you're doing?" Vivian's question stings, but I shrug it off.

"Yeah. I got it." I set the mugs on the table and open Grams' container of homemade hot chocolate mix. "Would you rather have tea?"

"Cocoa is good." Vivian's gaze fixes on my hands as I measure two scoops into each mug.

I'm distracted by the unguarded softness of her expression and miss the mug completely with the final scoop. Her eyes sparkle with amusement when she meets my gaze. In a flash, a mask of indifference replaces the friendly humor when her green eyes narrow as the corners of her mouth drop into a frown. So close.

After wiping up my mess and putting the final scoop into the mug, I retreat to the stove and stir the soup before pulling the whistling kettle from the heat. Determined not to be distracted by Vivian this time, I pour the boiling water into the mugs and check the soup once more.

A sound, suspiciously like a moan, reverberates off the small kitchen's walls and hits me square in the chest like an arrow piercing its target. I pinch my eyes closed and lean against the cabinet bracing myself against the need simmering deep beneath my collected exterior.

"God, I forgot how good her cocoa was." Another appreciative moan sends another pang of lust through me. "Are you okay?"

"Yeah," I choke out. "I'm fine." But I'm not okay. I'm far from it. Being in the same room with Vivian is physically painful at this point. Especially when she continues to make those illicit noises. I take three deep, calming breaths before focusing on transferring the soup from the pot to the bowls and sitting across from Vivian at the tiny kitchen table.

The goulash tastes exactly how I remember. Warm and rich, the flavors linger on my tongue. I flinch when another moan escapes Vivian's lips upon her first bite of the stew.

"Could you not make that sound?" I growl into my goulash.

Vivian's hand hovers over her bowl with a spoonful inches from her mouth. "What noise?" She takes another bite and holds my gaze before repeating the sound deep in the back of her throat.

My spoon clatters against the porcelain when I drop it. "Okay, Viv. I get it. You're still pissed at me after twenty years, but there's no reason for you to be a brat."

"Me? A brat?" She sets her spoon aside and glares across the table.

"I make one mistake and I'm the bad guy forever. Is that it?" I throw my hands up in defeat.

"A mistake? A mistake." Vivian sticks her tongue in her cheek, her face flaring a lovely shade of crimson. "I'm glad we cleared that up." She pushes away from the table, grabbing her bowl and her mug before retreating into the living room.

I lean back in my chair and run my hands through my hair, pulling so hard my scalp aches. "Infuriating little..." I take a deep breath and exhale to clear my mind. What the hell is wrong with me? We're adults. Why can't we talk about what happened and move on? I shake my head.

A chill settles over me and I finish my goulash alone. After washing the dishes, I check the thermostat before heading into the living room. Sixty degrees? That's pushing it. But the dial is set for sixty-five. Maybe the boiler went out?

When I enter the living room, I fight the draw of Vivian's presence. Instead, I grab my coat and step out into the storm to check on the boiler. Maybe the cold will calm me down.

CHAPTER FOUR

VIVIAN

My heart's still racing. I can't even finish my goulash. I stare longingly at the half empty bowl. My stomach revolts at the thought of eating any more. I'm afraid I might throw up. Guilt twists in the pit of my stomach. It was so delicious. Until Andrew went and ruined everything. Big surprise there.

It's not my fault I made those noises. Well, the first two times anyway. That last one, oh, that was on purpose. One hundred percent. He deserves it. After what he did to me, he deserves every ounce of my fury.

I bundle myself tighter in the blanket on the couch and stare at the lights on the Christmas tree. Does he though? That was twenty years ago. No one remembers what happened. No one cares. The voice in my mind pleads with my sense of reason. No. What he did was unforgivable, and now he's back, the gossip is bound to resurface with a vengeance. The more I argue with myself the more bitter it tastes. I tug the blanket tighter around my shoulders. Damn, it's cold in here.

The snow's still coming down hard. It's been five minutes since Andrew stomped through the living room and disappeared out into the winter storm. Maybe I should check on him?

No. Let the bastard freeze to death.

Really, Viv? That's how you're going to play it? I groan and bury my face in the blanket. Am I really this petty? Twenty years of hard feelings?

The warmth in his smile and his kind actions may redeem him in the moment, but he's still the same Andrew beneath the handsome, masculine, irresistible charm. Shit. I shift uncomfortably and push away any positive thoughts of him.

The silence burrows beneath my skin. I pull out my phone and press play on my Christmas playlist. The soft, soothing strains of Santa Baby comes through the speakers and fills the room. I lean back and close my eyes. I will not think about Andrew and his sexy smile and how he looks better than every fantasy I've ever had of him since I was thirteen.

With a bang, the front door swings open. Andrew stumbles inside covered in snow with his hands cupped around his mouth. He kicks the door closed behind him and leans against it.

"Everything okay?" I ask hesitantly.

"Boiler's dead." His hands muffle his voice, but I hear him clearly.

"So, what do we do?" I stand up, keeping the blanket wrapped around me.

"I'll make a fire and pray the pipes don't freeze." He picks up some gloves by the door and disappears back outside.

After a few trips, Andrew has a decent pile of wood stacked near the fireplace. I watch as he strips off his coat and gloves. His cheeks are pink from the cold and exertion. Those mesmerizing eyes are bright when they fix on me.

"Do you need help?" I ask feeling guilty I haven't offered already.

"Grab the lighter in the drawer beside the stove." He crouches beside the fireplace and cleans a space to build the base.

Rudolph the Red Nosed Reindeer blasts from my pocket as I head into the kitchen and retrieve the lighter. I hand it to him, and he stares up at me, his mouth pressed into a thin line.

"Are we five?" he asks.

"What?"

"Rudolph." He gestures to the music coming from my pocket. "Can you play something else?"

I hit next and unfortunately it's Mariah Carey's *All I Want for Christmas is You*. The look Andrew shoots me is full of pure hatred.

"Fine." I hit the button a few times until it settles on one of my favorite Christmas songs.

As soon as the song plays, Andrew groans. "Really? *Baby,*

It's Cold Outside?"

"What?" I shrug. "It's a good song."

"You don't find it offensive?" He glances over his shoulder at me.

"No. Why would I?" I'm sincerely curious since it's been one of my favorite holiday songs since I was a teen.

"There was a girl in the office who absolutely hated this song. Said it represented date rape and a man not respecting a woman's boundaries."

"You're kidding?" I think about the lyrics for a minute. "I mean, I can see where she's coming from, but it still doesn't make sense to me. The song comes from an era with different expectations and societal norms, so why would you try to put a contemporary context to a song like that?"

Andrew slumps against the fireplace and stares at me. His lips curl into a lopsided grin and my heart flips. "Good point."

"Well then, what's your favorite Christmas song? I'll play that one." I open the search bar in my app and wait. When he doesn't answer, I glance up. His furrowed brow and the scowl give me pause. "Do you have one?"

"No. I don't like Christmas music."

My jaw drops. "Are you serious?"

"Obviously. Why would I lie about that?"

"Because Christmas is obviously the best holiday of the year."

He frowns harder, if that's possible. "No, it's not."

I cross my arms and step closer, ignoring the warning bells going off in my head. His warm scent lures me closer and I wrangle control of my sanity to face him down. "Yes, it is."

"Why?" He stares down at me and I'm drowning in those eyes like I did when I was fifteen.

"Because holidays are a racket created by corporations to sell a shit ton of merchandise and capitalize on the sentimental emotions of the population." The strength in his voice plays at odds with the heat in his gaze. He's bluffing. I can see it. There's more here, but I know hell will freeze over before he lets me peel those layers back and expose the truth.

"Cynical much?" I jab him in the chest. The joyful strains of the Chipmunks fill the room and I grin.

"Not cynical." He pushes my hand away. We're not touching now, but the heat radiating of his body is damn near nuclear. "Just realistic. I spent the last fifteen years playing the marketing game. I know how this shit works. There's nothing holly or jolly about Christmas. It's a sucker's market, and I've learned to capitalize off of it."

Our eyes lock and a silent battle ignites between us. I lick my lips and wish I had the guts to take what I want from him. Reality is, I don't know what I want from him, and I still haven't forgiven him for what he did to me all those years ago. Or for running away and staying away for twenty years without so much as a phone call. Bastard.

I glare at him. "You're telling me you hate Christmas?"

"Yes."

"Why?"

He cocks his head. "Do I need a reason?"

"Yes." I prop my hands on my hips and the blanket drops to the floor. His gaze rakes over my body before settling on my mouth for a half a breath and then locking gazes.

"Because Christmas is bullshit." He turns and drops to his knees before the fireplace intent on building a fire.

I shiver and snatch my blanket from the floor. As I wrap it around my shoulders and collapse on the couch, I watch Andrew work. I didn't think it was possible to hate him more than I already did, but here we are. So much for trying to make the best of a bad situation.

CHAPTER FIVE

ANDREW

Irritated, I focus on the task before me and attempt to ignore the festive music slowly grating on my last exposed nerve. My response may have been harsh, but it wasn't inaccurate. Christmas, in my opinion, is bullshit. No need to sugar coat the truth.

Taking my time, I stack the small pieces of wood and light the tinder beneath it. Coaxing this fire to life is easier than coaxing a warm welcome from the ice queen sitting on the couch. An outsider would think I killed her entire family and left her orphaned and penniless on the streets. The reality was far less dramatic. I regret my youthful actions, but shame in admitting my own incompetence keeps me from rehashing the past.

Not that I need to do so. The furrow between her brows tells me she remembers everything in vivid high definition.

I blow on the embers until they take hold and burst into flame. After I'm sure the fire has taken hold, I add some larger pieces to the grate. Since the boiler's out, the fire serves as our only source of heat. In any other circumstances, being trapped with a gorgeous woman during a snowstorm would have been heaven.

Vivian pulls the blanket closer and shifts her gaze to the Christmas tree when I step away from the fireplace. I brush the dirt off my hands and retreat into the bathroom to clean up. In the bedroom, I grab a few heavy quilts Grams keeps in a large oak chest at the foot of her bed and head back into the living room.

I pause in the hallway at the sound of the Carol of the Bells.

It was Mom's favorite song. I shake the maudlin memories free. The glow of the Christmas lights plays across Vivian's features as she scans through her phone. Finally, she locks the screen and sets the device aside. Her heavy sigh echoes through the room.

"You cold?" I toss the blankets onto the armchair beside the tree.

She nestles deeper in the afghan draped around her. "No, I'm fine."

I nod and sit on the other end of the couch, pulling off my boots with a groan. The heat from the fire reaches into the room, curling around us in silence.

The song switches to the Twelve Days of Christmas. I scoff. I haven't heard that one in years.

"What?" Vivian searches my face.

"I don't think I've heard this song since I was a kid." I wince at the mention of the past and stretch my legs avoiding the topic further.

"You really hate Christmas?" Vivian's question hovers between us.

"I don't have any use for it." I shrug as though it's obvious.

"Why not?" she pries deeper. "It's a time for joy and celebration and family. We all need that."

I tip my gaze toward the ceiling and study the wooden beam running the length of the room. "I guess not everyone does."

"You'd rather be miserable all year long?"

"It's better than pretending. I'd rather not indulge in the lie that everything is sugar plums and fairy dust. Christmas isn't magical, it's make-believe. The whole holiday perpetuates an illusion of harmony and happiness. It's bullshit." I shrug.

"Wow, Andrew. I knew you could be a cocky asshole but not a cynical bastard. Did the city do that to you? I don't remember you being like this before you left for New York."

"People change, darlin'."

Vivian scoffs. "Don't darlin' me. You haven't changed. I think it was always there beneath the surface." She pauses pressing her fingertips to her lips. "You know those *Hallmark* holiday movies?"

I snort. "No, but I bet you've watched them all, haven't you?"

She glares at me. "The city slickers always discover the true meaning of Christmas in small towns."

"That's it, add to the delusion." I shake my head. "Where is this going?"

Vivian growls. "Never mind. You're a lost cause."

"Took you long enough to figure that out." The couch gives a little as I turn and lean closer. "Tell me the truth, Vivian. Are you still pissed about what happened between us?"

She gravitates away from me, pressing her back against the arm of the couch. "Why should I care what happened twenty years ago?"

"Because you've treated me like absolute shit since the moment I walked into your coffee shop." I wet my lips.

Her gaze catches the movement and those lovely eyes darken. "I have not."

"You have been completely antagonistic toward me. And I want to know why?"

"Back up, Andrew." She pushes her hand against my chest, and her touch brands me.

"No. I have questions, and I want answers." I hold my ground. The sweet scent of her soap and coffee swirls in my brain making me crave her more.

"If you kiss me, Andrew, so help me, God, I will punch you in the dick."

"It's not like this would be the first time for either of those things."

A smirk plays on her lips, but the humor doesn't reach her eyes. "Punching you in the dick was an accident, but this time it won't be."

"I shouldn't have crawled into bed with you that night." I'm playing with fire bringing up these memories, teasing the chemistry sizzling between us, but common sense and reason have completely abandoned me. I only want her to consume me.

"Your sister told me to take your bed." The pressure of her hand on my chest is steady. "We thought you were staying at a friend's house."

"I was supposed to, but plans changed." The night remains clear in my mind even through the haze of the cheap alcohol we'd been drinking. I stumbled into the basement to find my sister's extremely attractive best friend asleep in my bed. "My balls ached for a week afterwards."

"Served you right. You scared the shit out of me." Her voice softens on the last sentence.

"I apologized."

"So did I." She scowls. "But asking me to kiss it and make it better definitely crossed the line."

"What?" I shrug. "It was a joke. I was kidding."

"Being a seventeen-year-old jerk didn't give you permission to be a perv. I was fourteen, Andrew. Fourteen."

"A fourteen-year-old who had a crush on her best friend's older brother." I play the card knowing it's a gamble.

Her jaw drops, but she composes herself quickly. "Every girl in school had a crush on you. Every freaking one."

"Yeah, and?" Haunting echoes of a long-ago conversation with my sister tugs at my brain. I shove it away. "It doesn't change the fact I'm right. You had a crush on me. Admit it."

"Why does it matter?" Vivian pushes me away as she stands and stares into the fire. "That was twenty years ago. I'm not the same person I was." She faces me once more. "And neither are you."

"You're right." I shoot to my feet before I can question my own actions and pull her into my arms. Her pink lips part in surprise. Those intoxicating green eyes lock with mine and I tighten my grip as I kiss her the way I've wanted to since the moment I tasted her all those years ago. Dark chocolate and peppermint linger on her tongue, and I'm swept away in the moment.

CHAPTER SIX

VIVIAN

One minute I can breathe, and the next I'm bombarded with sensation and emotions I thought I'd long since banished to the past. Andrew's kiss overwhelms me. I cling to him, tilting my head to allow him access. He tastes like the hot cocoa and something darker, more visceral. His grip tightens, holding me against him, and even though I threatened to punch him if he kissed me, I concede, if only for a sample.

His hand cups my jaw, fingertips brushing my earlobe. I sigh against his mouth and shift my weight into him. It's been too long since I've been held in such a way. My ex-husband wasn't known for his tenderness or passion. But even since the divorce, there's been a distinct absence of spark when it came to intimacy. Andrew's presence in my shop tossed a lit match to a storehouse of fireworks. It was only a matter of time before everything exploded.

"Oh, Viv." His whisper brushes my ear and I drop the blanket to wrap my arms around him. We stumble back until he collapses onto the couch, pulling me with him.

The warm fire, soft twinkling of lights, and delicate strains of Christmas music adds the perfect setting to this intimate moment. Until the music cuts to a song that sounds vaguely like my ringtone.

Andrew's wandering hands go still on my hips as his mouth wanders the length of my neck. "Are you going to answer that?"

"Yeah." I grab my phone, still straddling the man I swore to hate until my dying day. *Charlotte* flashes across the screen. "Shit." I meet Andrew's curious gaze when I answer the phone.

"Hey, honey."

"Mom, where are you?" my daughter's voice booms through the speaker, loud enough for anyone in a five-foot radius of my phone to hear her. "The festival has been cancelled, but no one seems to know where you are." I hear the condemnation in her tone. She's hurt I didn't call her.

Andrew's eyes widen and he mouths the word *Mom* like it's a question and the thought never occurred to him. I hold my hand up and shift my weight to slide off his lap. His grip tightens on my waist, and he shakes his head.

"I'm sorry, hon. I ran an errand with a friend, and we got stuck in the storm." I bite my lip and curse myself for not being open with her, but she deserves to hear it in person, not over the phone. "I'll be home tomorrow in time for dinner. The roads should be clear by then. Dad has you until six."

"Yeah, I know." She heaves a dramatic sigh. "It's...Niki saw you driving out of town with some guy. Are you okay? Where are you?"

"Oh, well, Andrew's an old friend from high school. He's visiting his grandma for the holiday. Ruth, you remember her from the shop."

Andrew's left brow arches in question but thankfully he remains silent. Unfortunately, I can feel every hard inch of him beneath me which makes conversation with my daughter extremely difficult. I rest my hand against his chest and shoot him an unspoken warning.

"Ruth?" Charlotte chuckles. "Well, that explains why your phone location shows her cabin." She pulls the phone away from her mouth and shouts to someone else. "She's at Ruth's, Dad. Calm down!"

I shake my head. Of course, my ex would have to stick his nose in it. I forgot I had turned on location services for my phone. It was a relatively innocent trade off to turn on my location in order to have access to Charlotte's as well. Andrew seems amused by the whole conversation. I try to pull away, but he wraps his arms around my waist drawing me against him. When his lips touch my neck, I lose all coherent thought.

"Dad said he'll pick you up right now." Charlotte's voice

barely registers.

"Not tonight. The snow's coming down pretty...heavy. Um, I'll call tomorrow if I can't make it down the mountain." My hand wraps around Andrew's throat. *Stop!* I mouth the warning.

Andrew ceases his torture and I drop my hand.

"Okay, I'll let Dad know. I love you." Charlotte sounds relieved.

"Love you too." I hang up the phone and toss it aside when the Christmas music resumes.

"How old is she?" Andrew asks, his fingertips pressing against my spine.

"Fourteen." The fact that she's the same age I was when Andrew climbed into bed with me doesn't escape my notice. It doesn't escape his either, if his guilty expression is anything to go by.

"I'm sorry, Viv."

"Sorry for what?" I offer a sympathetic smile. "I should have told you about Charlotte."

"No, I mean, well, yes, for being an ass while you were on the phone with your daughter." He shifts uncomfortably. "I'm sorry for the way I treated you when we were kids."

"You mean the way you teased me relentlessly behind closed doors and ignored me in front of your friends."

He cups my face in his hand and draws me closer until our breaths intertwine. "Yes, for that. But I'm more sorry I didn't realize the truth sooner."

"What truth?" My breasts press against his chest as he eliminates any space between us.

"Remember the Christmas dance my senior year?"

Shame burns across my cheeks as the memory rushes into my mind's eye. "The one where we got caught under the mistletoe in front of the whole school?"

"Yeah." He groans as though the memory pains him as much as it does me.

"Are you apologizing for making me look like a lovestruck idiot in front of the whole school?" Even after so much time has passed, the memory stings like an open wound doused with salt.

"I never meant to hurt you, Viv." He scowls. "If I had known it was your first kiss...how you felt about me, I wouldn't have done it. It was a mistake."

"Kissing me was a mistake?"

"No, stealing that first from you was. It was supposed to be special. You deserved better, and I ruined it for you."

"The kiss was perfect." I wrap my arms around Andrew's neck, his warmth grounding me. "What you did after was unforgivable."

Andrew's brow furrows in confusion. "Wait? What did I do after that?"

"You told all your friends how easy I was. How you had your own little pet willing to do anything you wanted. They called me a slut." The expression of horror on Andrew's face makes me pause.

"Viv. I never said anything like that. They harassed me for weeks about what happened at the Christmas dance, but I never said anything to disrespect you." He paused. "Is that why you stopped coming over? Stopped hanging out with my sister?"

"I couldn't face you, Andrew. I just wanted it to end." I shake my head and try to hide my face. It all seems so fucking stupid now. But I can't stop the tears from coming. "I was both relieved and heartbroken when you graduated and left Coppany."

He tips my chin up and I'm smitten with him all over again with a single look. "Viv. I'm so sorry." He kisses my lips softly. "Why didn't you tell me?"

"You could have come to me too, you know?" I swipe the tears away with the back of my hand.

"We both fucked up." He brushes a tear from the corner of my eye.

"It seems so stupid now." I laugh. "Twenty years, wasted."

"Not wasted." He smiles. "Just delayed."

This time when he kisses me, I'm more than ready...I'm willing. Andrew wraps his hand in my hair and pulls my head back as he kisses down the column of my neck.

"What do you want, Viv?" He presses his mouth over my

pulse and sucks gently.

"For you to finish what you started." My body's on fire, and I don't care that we're snowed in at Ruth's cabin in the living room. I want him to lay claim to me in every possible way.

CHAPTER SEVEN

ANDREW

With those simple words, she sets me on fire. Vivian grinds against me and the last remaining hesitation evaporates from in my mind. My hands explore her back, sliding beneath the soft fabric of her sweater and ghosting over her bare skin. She threads her fingers through my hair and pulls until my head tips back and our gazes lock.

The soft glow of Christmas lights reflects in her eyes. God, I missed her. Even as a kid, she had the most striking green eyes. I'd be lying if I said I hadn't imagined her pinning me down with a hungry look. But I never imagined how hard it would make me.

I buck my hips against hers, and she tightens her grip on me. A small gasp slips between her parted lips.

My hands take control and pull the sweater over her skin. She tugs it over her head and tosses it aside. My gaze drifts over her bare skin following the gentle curve of her breasts cradled in red fabric. I brush my fingertips across her breasts and around until I unclasp the band. The fabric falls away and she tosses it with the discarded top.

I've never been a breast man, but Vivian's revelation converts me. My lips caress the soft skin until I capture a pert nipple between my teeth. She holds my head steady as I explore her breasts, laving attention on one and then the other until her nipples are tight and sensitive. She shivers as my breath brushes the tips.

"Andrew, please." Her breathy plea makes me harder. I didn't think that was physically possible.

"I'm taking my time with you, Viv." I shift our positions until she's lying on the couch. I stand up to strip off the layers of clothing, and she wiggles out of what remains of her own.

My hand hovers over the buckle of my belt when I see the banquet before me. If I thought she was gorgeous as a teenager, she's fucking stunning now. She's all soft, inviting curves. The delicate, faded marks across her abdomen and hips draw my attention down to where her fingers brush the dark curls between her thighs.

Distracted by the sight, I climb onto the couch and draw her thighs around me. My lips trace a path over her stomach and down to her sex. When I take her in my mouth, her moan sends a bolt of lust through me. I wish I'd have taken my jeans off now. Pushing the thought away, I redouble my efforts and devour her. My tongue works against her clit and she grasps my head as her thighs tighten around me. When I slip my finger inside, a soft curse slips from her guarded lips.

"Holy fuck." She moans as I move my finger and my tongue in tandem. "Yes. More. Please." Her plea drives me into action. Fast and harder, until I feel her tense beneath my mouth.

Vivian on the brink of orgasm is by far the most beautiful sight I've seen in a long time. Her flushed skin, my hands fisted in her hair, back arching against the couch, hips moving against my mouth as she tries to ride my hand. The incoherent words bubbling from her mouth make me grin with pride. I love that I can make her fall apart so completely. When she finally comes, I suck her clit between my teeth to draw out her pleasure.

"Andrew! Fuck," she shouts, and I'm thankful we're alone in a cabin miles from the nearest neighbor. I want to hear her scream my name over and over until she's hoarse and trembling.

I soften my touch as she shivers beneath me. When I sit back and lick my fingers, her dazed expression ignites into hunger through the aftermath of her orgasm.

"You're evil." She tosses a small pillow at me.

I bat it away and stand up. "I didn't hear any complaints."

"Proud of yourself, are you?" She lounges gracefully, drawing her fingers across her bare stomach.

Instead of responding, I smirk and grab a blanket from the pile I brought in from the bedroom earlier. I lay it on the floor in front of the fireplace and reach for my belt.

Her gaze darkens and before I can unfasten the buckle, she's on her knees before me. The soft grip around my cock as she slips me free is almost enough to make me come. She licks her lips and presses a kiss to the tip.

"Oh, sweetheart, as much as I want to see my cock in your mouth, let's save that for later." I push my jeans and underwear down to the floor before kicking them aside. They hit the Christmas tree knocking three ornaments to the floor. "Shit."

Vivian laughs. A sound so rich and pure, I'm struck stupid by the sound of it. It's the first time I've heard her laugh since we were kids. Her smile shines brighter than the brightest star in the sky. The force of it throws my heart back against my ribs. Fuck, she's gorgeous.

I drop to my knees and kiss her, hard and fast, stealing her smile with my lips and branding it on my mind. She wraps her arms around me, and without hesitation, she darts her tongue across mine, tasting and searching. I wrap my hand in her hair and tug. She bares her neck to me and gasps when I gently nip along the length of it.

"Viv. You're killing me."

"I didn't do anything yet." Her breathy laugh dies on a moan when I drag my teeth along her collar bone.

"I have a confession." At this point, the truth may be irrelevant, but she deserves to hear it. I'm drunk on her. The more I get, the more I want. And I want everything.

She pulls me up and seals my lips into silence. A long, sensual kiss leaves me swaying against her. "I thought confession time was over. This is sexy time." She kisses me again.

I cup her face between my hands and put space between us. Her swollen lips turn down in an exaggerated pout. "The Christmas dance." My heart races. "When I kissed you under the mistletoe and played it off?"

Hurt flashes in her eyes. "Yeah."

"I didn't mean to hurt you. I had to push you away." I lick my lips and curse myself for being an ass. "I wanted you. So desperately. But you were my sister's best friend and I was about to graduate. You still had three years left." I pinch my eyes closed. "I fucked up. I'm sorry."

I feel a gentle touch against my cheek and open my eyes. Vivian's smiling again and she's so fucking beautiful my heart threatens to break.

"You did." She rubs her thumb across my lower lip. "It took me years to realize it wasn't something I did." She grips my jaw in her hand. "I deserved better. And for years, I wanted to rip you apart for hurting me."

"Explains the cold reception when I walked into the coffee shop earlier."

Her gaze softens. "Seeing you walk into my life after twenty years of being absent." She sighs. "It tore open a wound I thought healed long ago."

"You had every right to hold a grudge for the way I treated you. Pushing you away. Not being there when you needed me." I settle my hands on her hips and pull her naked body flush against mine. "I was an asshole. You were right to hate me."

Her eyes flutter closed for a moment before she responds. "That's the problem, Andrew. I never hated you, even after you pulled that shit and bailed." She wraps her arms around me and rests her head against my chest.

A blend of uncertainty and hope takes root in my mind. The heat of her body sinks into me, and I'm finding it difficult to focus on anything but burying my cock in her and making her mine. Regrets be damned, I finally have her in my arms and there's no way in hell I'm letting her go.

CHAPTER EIGHT

VIVIAN

What the hell is wrong with me? I'm naked on the floor with Andrew two seconds away from having sex and I'm confessing what...I've loved him for twenty some years. I shake the thoughts from my head and hide my face against his chest.

I almost said it. *Shit*. I almost told him. *No*. This is purely physical, whatever this is. A chemical, hormonal anomaly, pheromones or whatever, that takes over and overrides any fucking common sense the moment I encounter someone who's hot as sin and I want to jump them. That's it. Twenty years should have erased the crush I harbored for Andrew over my entire teenage existence. And yet, here I am, a breath away from admitting I love him, and I always have.

The silence stretches between us and I wonder if he's going to change his mind. After the mind blowing orgasm he gave me, I want to return the favor. But as much as I want to blow his mind, I'd rather take my time teasing him later. His cock brushes against my stomach and I smile at knowing I have such an effect on him.

"Viv." His fingers slide over my hips and his palm splays over my lower back. The husky sound of his voice makes me ache for his mouth on me again, his talented tongue making me come over and over.

I push him down to the floor. His brow arches and the flicker of firelight casts shadows across his face. He's dark and drowning in need, it's etched deep in his expression. He lays down and I straddle his stomach, my clit brushes his cock and he hisses.

Andrew grips my hips so tight, I can't help but hope it leaves bruises. I brace my hands on his chest and rub myself up and down his length. His head tips back, eyes closed, mouth open. Empowerment rushes through me.

His eyes shoot open, hazed with desire, and he licks his lips. "Shit. Protection." He moves to push me off him when I pin him down by the wrists.

"Are you clean?" Our lips are a breath apart, and he stills beneath me.

"Yes." His body tenses. "You?"

"I haven't had sex in years, Andrew." I cock my head.

"What about..." He takes a breath. "You know."

"I've got it covered." I grin, knowing what he's asking but reveling in the way it makes him uncomfortable. "I didn't bring any condoms, and I doubt you did either. I'm going to take a stab at it and say Ruth doesn't keep them in her medical cabinet."

Andrew groans in disgust. "Please, don't. I'd really like to continue this, but if we talk about my grandma's sex life, I may be flaccid for the foreseeable future."

I kiss him hard and his cock jumps against my inner thigh. "We're good then?"

"Fuck yes." He cups my face and we're lost in the heat of passion once more.

I slide my hand between us and slip him inside me. He's hot and hard and deep. I inhale sharply as he drives even deeper. The whimper that escapes my throat is fucking inhuman. When he thrusts, I rock my hips and cling to him.

"That's it, baby. Ride me."

Shit. It's like he knows how much I like dirty talk. I find a rhythm and he meets me beat for beat until we're both panting and gasping with need. When he puts the pad of his finger against my clit, I moan as the sensations multiply. My climax lingers out of reach and I guide him, faster and faster as we ride to the top of the mountain and I fall over the edge of the cliff into an abyss of pure pleasure.

I scream his name as I come, and he grips my hips tight, firing off a rapid succession of thrusts until he finds his own release. I'm lost in the dazed aftermath and collapse against his overheated body. Sticky and sated, we lay on the blanket before the fire.

The delicate strains of Christmas music filter through the room. I forgot it was still playing. The glow of the tree casts multi-colored streaks of light across our skin as the flames flicker from the fire casting shadows. I burrow closer to him and he wraps his arm around me securing me to his side. I'm half asleep when he finally speaks.

"Wow."

I prop myself up on my elbow. "Wow, what?"

"I wasn't expecting that." He studies my face, his gaze occasionally drifting to my breast resting against his side.

"To get laid?" I grin.

"Well, yes." Andrew pauses. "But I wasn't expecting to see you at all."

"I live here. Have all my life." I tease him. "It's a small town, remember?"

"Yes, but..." He's searching for words; I can see the wheels spinning in his mind. "You're smart and resourceful. Why are you still here? I thought you'd go off to college and move away."

"Like you did?" I shake my head. "I couldn't leave. Dad needed help at the store. Then I got married. Then Charlotte came along." I shrug not really wanting to go into details. Not like this, naked and post-coital. "This is home. I couldn't leave."

Andrew nods, his fingertips brushing over my side, back and forth. "I understand."

"What took you so long to come back?" I smile softly but my heart aches at the thought of all the wasted time.

"After the shit show of a miserable year we had, I needed to see Grams. This whole year has been a massive collection of disappointments. When Grams called and asked me to come home, I knew it was time." He sighs and stares at the ceiling. "I felt guilty she was here alone."

"She wasn't alone." I place my hand over his heart. "We took care of her. She's family."

He meets my gaze and I see the gratefulness in their depths. "I appreciate that."

"Don't beat yourself up." My voice softens. "This year has

been shitshow for everyone." I push aside the memories of all the drama and disappointments I experienced myself during the chaos and uncertainty. "I'm glad you came back. Ruth is so proud of you. She brags about you to all her friends."

"She acts like I own a million-dollar company, not work for one."

"You're successful and brilliant. She's proud of you." I chuckle. "How is work, anyway?"

"Different. Better. Well, one of my bosses finally got married. Thank God. The one good thing that happened this year. He finally has a life outside of work which makes it easier on the rest of us. Gave us a whole week off for Christmas too, if you can believe it."

"That's nice of him."

"His wife sent me an invitation to their first Christmas party as a couple." He cringes. "I see enough of Ben at work. I don't want to deal with him off the clock if I don't have to."

"Hard ass?" I prompt.

"Workaholic." He growls. "Doesn't know when to turn it off. I hope his wife distracts him now, at least until the merger goes through next spring."

"He sounds like a trip." I laugh.

"They both are." He pulls me closer. "Penelope reminds me a little of you."

"Your boss's wife?"

He nods. "She's sassy and fun. Just like you used to be."

"Used to be?"

"Still are." Andrew grins. "I'm glad I came back. I needed this."

I lay down against his chest and close my eyes. My heart full and my mind spinning. "So did I," I murmur against his skin.

As we lay in silence, I fight against the war threatening to consume me inside. Andrew has his life in New York, and I have mine here. How will we make this work? Does he even want to? I bite my tongue from putting voice to the words that need to be said. I love him, and I want him in my life.

But can it work?

CHAPTER NINE

ANDREW

Sometime later, hours it feels like, I wake to find the room cold and the fire burned down to embers. The blanket tucked around us isn't warm enough to stave off the chill settling in the cabin. After pressing a soft kiss to her forehead, I disentangle myself from her sleeping form and tuck the warm afghan around Vivian.

I wrap a blanket around myself and stoke the fire back to life. The heat radiates through me banishing the chill. Something vibrates near my foot. I wrestle my jeans from beneath me and pull my phone from the pocket.

Grams. The name flashes across the screen. I quickly rise and head for the bathroom as not to wake Vivian. Once I'm inside, I shut the door.

"Hey, Grams."

"Andrew. Is everything okay? How's Vivian?" Despite the hour, Grams sounds wide awake.

"Grams," I glance at my watch to confirm my suspicion. "It's after eleven. Why aren't you in bed?"

"Julia invited a few of the other ladies to stay too, so we're making the best of it. Poker and glühwein." Grams chuckles. "Oh, pipe down will you? It's Andrew." Her voice echoes in the background as she speaks to someone on her end.

I roll my eyes. "As long as you're okay." If there's one thing I know about Grams, she can take care of herself. At eighty-two, I can only hope to have half the energy and tenacity she possesses. Heaven help anyone who tries to tell her what to do. I learned that lesson long ago.

"I'm fine. Don't you worry your head about me." The noise

behind her fades. "Everything going okay up there?"

The question makes me pause. Is she fishing for something? A tidbit of information, perhaps. As appreciative as I was of Grams giving us an excuse to be alone together, I'm even more convinced this was a set up. I shake my head.

"We're fine, Grams. I had to start a fire. The boiler's dead."

"I figured it might die." Grams sounds thoughtful. "Right before you showed up, I put a call in to have someone check it out in the morning." She sighs. "I was hoping it would hold out until then."

I pinch the bridge of my nose. "Good to know, Grams."

"Are you two going to be warm enough? You may have to bundle up together in the living room or something."

Vivid memories of Vivian and I doing much more than bundling up together in the living room flash through my mind. My blood instantly heats, and my cock demands an encore. Shit. I ignore my body's demands and focus on the conversation with Grams.

"We're fine. I've got it under control."

"I'm sure you do," Grams replies slowly like a wise village elder full of mystical secrets.

"Grams..." I open my mouth to ask her if she had ulterior motives to this whole get my medication bullshit, but she cuts me off.

"I gotta run. Mildred's dealt the next hand. I love you. Goodnight."

"Goodnight, Grams. Love you too."

The phone disconnects and I'm left staring at my reflection in the cold bathroom. I splash some freezing water on my face after using the toilet and wrap the blanket tighter around me.

The warmth from the fire has already started filtering through the house again. Thank goodness it's a small enough space.

The blanket lays haphazardly across Vivian's bare form. She must have shifted in her sleep. My gaze drifts over a bare foot, along her leg, up over her thigh, across her stomach and one bared breast, until it finally settles on Vivian's sleeping face. My heart seizes in my chest and I double over from the impact. She's fucking gorgeous.

And she's mine. All mine.

The thought slams into me out of nowhere. I blink twice, still fixated on the woman at my feet. There's an undeniable truth to it even though I can't for the life of me figure out when the fuck it happened. Then it clicks. I've always known. I love Vivian. I did twenty years ago just as much as I do now. Time and distance did nothing to diminish the emotion burning a hole in my chest.

We've finally figured out what went wrong and how well we fit together. I groan at the persistent press of my cock bobbing against the blanket in agreement. I can't help but wonder where it goes from here. Is there a future for us together?

Vivian stirs and her intoxicating green gaze locks with mine. A sleepy smile crosses her lips as she stretches, making the blanket shift over her pale skin. "Hey."

"Hey."

She cocks her head and studies me. "Something wrong?"

"Nope." I point to the fire. "Just added some more wood and used the bathroom."

"I was wondering where you disappeared to." She chuckles. "I could've sworn I heard you talking to someone."

"Grams called to check on us. I didn't want to wake you." I toss the phone onto the couch and drop down beside Vivian, pulling her against my chest.

She nuzzles against my shoulder and heaves a contented sigh I feel in my soul. "Is she okay?"

"Yeah. She's playing poker and drinking glühwein." I scoff at the image it puts in my head.

"Oh yeah. That's a regular Christmas tradition with her. Normally Christmas Eve, but I guess it works tonight too." She laughs when she sees the look of confusion on my face. "What, you think she sits home and knits all the time?"

I lay my head back and stare at the ceiling. "No, but I never really thought about Grams doing something so un-grandmotherly."

"Now you're making shit up." Vivian smooths her hand across my stomach beneath the blanket. "Un-grandmotherly? What exactly should grandmothers do?"

"I don't know. Knit? Play bingo? Bake cookies? Go to Bible study? Visit with friends?"

"It is possible for her to do all those things on top of other things she enjoys and still be grandmotherly." Vivian props herself up. Her dark hair creates a curtain around her face.

All thought of Grams fades into the background. Vivian consumes my attention completely. I want to wrap my hands in her hair and pull, exposing her neck and teasing her with my mouth until she begs me to take her again.

She draws her lip between her teeth. "You're not thinking about your grandma anymore."

I shake my head.

"Good." She drops a kiss to the center of my chest, over my heart and draws the blankets down pressing soft kisses in its wake. When she reaches my cock, I'm hard and so fucking ready for her. She grasps it in her palm and strokes.

My hips thrust up involuntarily and my head falls back. I squeeze my eyes closed and let the sensations pulse through me.

When her hot tongue brushes the tip, I fist my hands in the blanket beneath me. "Fuck, baby, that's it."

I glance down in time to see my cock disappear between her lips. She's between my thighs, my cock buried deep in her throat. It's enough to make me come right there. I groan her name and then lose myself completely as she sucks.

A wash of pleasure courses through me as she moves, up and down, her mouth and hands making obscene noises with every stroke. It's so fucking hot. She draws it out, faster and then slower, teasing me to the point of madness. Bringing me to the point of climax only to deny me any kind of release. I catch her watching me through her lashes as she works, gauging my reaction.

She winks and I can't take it any longer.

"Shit, let me come, baby."

With a press of her fingers against the base of my cock, she sucks me deep, fast, and hard. Two strokes, and I'm tumbling over the edge. She swallows every last drop, milking me dry, until I'm twitching on her tongue.

Satisfied with her handywork, she climbs up my body and presses a salty kiss to my lips. I lounge for a moment to recover, drunk on her masterful touch.

"Where'd..." I lick my lips and clear my throat. "Where'd you learn that witchcraft?"

"Reading." She grins.

"Bullshit. You don't learn that from a book." I instinctively hate any man who's experienced her mouth in that way. Jealousy wrangles its way into my subconscious. I push it away and wrap my arms around her.

"Well, I read a lot of romance novels." She threads her hands in my hair and kisses me hard.

"Got a lot of book boyfriends, do you?" I tease between playful bites.

"Three or four new ones every week." She moans when I roll her onto her back and pin her hands to the floor.

"One man isn't enough to satisfy you, huh?"

She shakes her head. "Never."

I press my thigh against her pussy. Wet and hot. She groans and arches against me.

"Please." She licks her lips.

"Can your book boyfriends give you this?" I drink her in. Every flush, every whimper, every moan, every climax, they belong to me. All of it. All of her. Vivian belongs to me.

Chapter Ten

Vivian

I toss my head from side to side as he grinds against my clit. My arms are useless with my wrists pinned beneath his hands. His body cages mine. His piercing eyes are molten with need. Desire pulses between us. It's hot. So fucking hot.

I arch against him, wanting more friction. More contact. He presses down harder, preventing me from taking what I need. I shouldn't have teased him, prodding him with jabs about book boyfriends and blow job witchcraft. If I didn't know better, I'd say he was jealous. But they're only fictional...all of them. He punishes me by denying me the pleasure I crave almost as much as I crave his affection.

"No." Breathy pants escape my lips. "Please, Andrew."

"Do you want to come, sweetheart?" He whispers against my breast as his tongue brushes over my nipple.

I gasp at the burst of sensation and arch my hips. "Yes, please."

"Tell me exactly what you want me to do to you." He leans close, his eyes dark as a winter storm. His cock brushes against my thigh, hard once more.

"Fuck me." I arch up until my breasts graze his chest. "I want you so deep inside me I can't tell where I end and you begin."

He growls, guttural and possessive, before releasing my wrists and capturing my lips in a bruising kiss. I thread my fingers through his hair and pull him down against me. He devours my mouth as though branding me.

I slide my thighs open and he fits himself to me. Without effort, he thrusts inside and my world blanks. All I see is him. All I feel is him. Just like before, we're caught up in a maelstrom of passion oblivious to anything beyond this moment.

Our hips find a rhythm that mimic our tongues. I can't help but writhe against him. I need more, closer, faster, hotter.

He quickens his pace and presses two fingers to my clit. My hips buck at the burst of pressure, seeking the elusive pleasure I know he's more than willing to deliver.

"Yes, baby. That's it." He swallows my whimpers as he drives deeper into me.

I wrap my legs around him and push us both to the limit. The heat overwhelms me. Sweat slickened skin and the scent of him sends my mind into a frenzy. I draw his lower lip between my teeth and bite down.

He growls and punishes me with another forceful kiss. "Go ahead, Viv. Mark me. Make me yours." His fingers quicken their circles over my clit, and I cry out as my climax rushes toward me.

My teeth sink into his shoulder and pleasure pulses through me. Wave after wave of bliss tingling through every extremity as I come.

Andrew's groan tells me he's found his own release.

We lay in silence, stuck together, the scent of sex hanging in the air.

"Holy shit." I murmur as my mind slowly regains function.

"You can say that again." He rolls to the side and pulls me against him. His fingers brush my hair away from my face.

Guilt twists inside me. He needs to know what he does to me, how I feel about him. I deserve to know if this has a happy ending or if it's only wishful thinking and a one night stand.

"Andrew." My voice isn't as strong as I thought it would be. Damn it.

"Yeah, sweetheart."

My heart pounds at the simple term of endearment he's probably using casually. I sit up and look down at him. He's so handsome. Shit.

His brow furrows. "Something wrong?"

"What are we doing?" It's direct. I curse myself for not being more honest, but I don't want it to be awkward.

"Besides having amazing sex?" He smiles and I melt.

"Yes. Besides the obvious." I fidget with the blanket corner and avoid his gaze.

He grasps my chin and forces me to meet his gaze. "What do you want?"

"I want this to not be over tomorrow." I sigh knowing how ridiculous this sounds. "I love you, Andrew. I always have." I shrug. "You're successful with a great job in the city, and there's no way I would ask you to give that up. But I like this. Us. Together."

"I like it too." He rubs his thumb along my jaw.

"What do we do with it then? I mean. I have my life here, and you have your life there." I raise my hands in defeat as though it makes all the sense in the universe why this won't work.

Andrew sits up and grasps my shoulders. "Hey, this can work if we want it to." The tender expression mixed with the afterglow of sex softens me.

"How?" I grasp his arm.

"I don't know." He hangs his head and I can tell he's as baffled as I am. When he finally looks at me, I see the determination in his eyes. "Whatever happens, I want you to know, this wasn't a one-time deal for me. I love you too, and I want to make this work."

I can't breathe. The onslaught of emotion chokes me. He takes me in his arms and hugs me close. Together we sit there, unable to break through whatever has coalesced. A deal, an understanding, a bond...it doesn't matter. It's between us. I drink it in and relax knowing there will be an agreement of some kind at the end of all of this. But for now, it's the two of us. I can live with that.

We sit together, intertwined and sated, naked before the fire in his grandmother's house. Tomorrow we'll figure it out, but tonight, it's just the two of us. And for once, I'm okay with not knowing what the future will bring.

"Let's get some sleep." Andrew throws a couple more logs on the fire before we retire and wraps a blanket around us as we find a comfortable position on the floor in front of the fire. I settle against him and rest my head on his chest, his arm wrapped protectively around me.

Safe and secure...not to mention loved. That's exactly how I feel as I drift off to sleep.

"I love you, Andrew," I murmur.

He kisses my brow and holds me tight. "I love you too, Viv."

Chapter Eleven

Andrew

Something echoes in the back of my head. The rhythmic tempo grows louder and louder until I'm ripped from the depths of sleep.

Bang. Bang. Bang. "Vivian! Where the hell are you?" a man shouts at the front door.

"Oh shit." Vivian scrambles to her feet wrapping the blanket around her. Before I can even ask what the hell is going on, she motions for me to be quiet. "One minute," she shouts as the banging resumes. Her gaze shifts to me. "Get dressed."

We're dressed within minutes. Probably because the house is freezing cold and unsuited for lounging naked. The fire must have gone out early this morning. I kneel down to start another as Vivian runs to the door and opens it.

"Nick, what the hell are you doing here?" Vivian's voice is low and steady.

"Ruth asked me to check on the boiler. She said you got snowed in up here."

I ignore the jealousy twisting in my gut at the familiarity between Vivian and Nick. The embers are warm beneath my hand as I build another fire.

"Yeah. We did. How bad are the roads?"

"Bad. There's no way you're getting off this hill in that car." Nick's comment smacks of condescension. "Who's is it anyway?"

"Ruth's grandson, Andrew. He's an old friend."

"Yeah, I remember. He was a few years ahead of us." Nick clears his throat.

The fire sparks to life as the conversation draws closer.

When I turn, Nick and Vivian are behind me. Nick's gaze drifts to the fireplace and our eyes lock. Yeah, I remember him even though he's older, broader, and sporting a full beard. Played JV ball, followed my sister and Vivian around like a lost puppy. I slowly rise to my feet.

"Hey, Nick." I offer my hand.

"Andrew." He shakes it before letting his attention drift back to Vivian. "I'm gonna take a look at the boiler. If you need a lift back to town, I brought the truck."

I can't help but bristle at the statement. Yes, my Audi isn't the best on slick, snow covered mountain roads, but I can't very well park a full-size truck in Brooklyn, can I?

"That'd be great." Vivian smiles at Nick.

I think I'm going to be sick.

As soon as Nick heads outside and around the back of the house, I round on Vivian. "What was that about?"

"What?" She blinks twice, her lips twitching.

"Don't give me that bull shit. What's up with you and Nick? He's still smitten over you after all these years." I rake my hand through my hair.

Vivian folds her arms across her chest. "Andrew, are you jealous of Nick?"

"No. Why? Should I be?" I want to kiss that smirk right off her face and make her forget Nick's even alive.

"Yes. I mean, he is my ex-husband."

The edges of my vision darken. "He's what?"

"My ex. We were married for ten years, Andrew." She crosses the distance between us and settles her hand over my heart, fisting the fabric in her hand. "Green's not a good color on you, lover. Don't worry. Nick and I share a daughter and a friendly agreement, but that's it."

The thought of Nick having sex with Vivian sends my emotions into a fury. I clench my teeth and nod. "I'm not jealous."

"Bullshit. Your poker face is terrible." She cradles my face in her warm palm. "I meant what I said last night. I love you."

I wrap her in my arms and kiss her, hard. This kiss is

different. More desperate, more hungry, like both of us realize our time together is limited and we need one last fix before retreating into our own worlds. The room fades into the distance and all that remains is us, bound in this moment.

A cough from the doorway breaks us apart. I hold Vivian against me and glare at Nick standing in the doorway. "I need to run down to my shop in town for a part. I can have this up and running when I get back." His gaze settles on Vivian. "Need a lift into town?"

"Yeah." She presses a soft kiss to my lips before grabbing her coat by the door and slipping on her shoes. "Can you give me one minute? I'll meet you in the truck."

"No problem." Nick nods to me before he disappears into the winter wonderland outside where his Ford pickup is idling.

Vivian takes my hand and intertwines our fingers. "I need to check on my shop and pick up my daughter tonight." She chews on her lip. "I'll give you a call later, okay?"

My heart sinks. As much as I didn't want to admit it, I'm thankful the storm forced our hands. Being alone with Vivian was amazing, but I know she has her responsibilities, like I do. "Yeah, no problem. Go. Take care of your stuff. You know where to find me."

Vivian kisses me one last time. The taste of her makes me want to drag her inside and bury myself inside her again and again. When she pulls away, we're both a bit breathless.

"Go. Nick's waiting."

She nods and turns to leave without a goodbye. I don't say it either, because I'm afraid everything that happened will disintegrate into the air and vanish forever.

I wave as they head down the driveway and lock myself in the cabin. Shit. My stomach growls. I ignore the pile of blankets in front of the fireplace, grab my phone, and head into the kitchen. The phone's dead. I borrow Grams' charger, complete with a twelve foot cord, and plug it in so it will charge while I make coffee and eggs.

The scent of coffee percolating fills the air. I inhale deep and turn on the stove, tossing a few eggs into the hot iron skillet.

My phone vibrates. I forgot to turn the ringer on again.

Grams lights up the screen.

"Hey, Grams. Hope you won big last night." I prop the phone on my shoulder while I flip the eggs.

"I did. That'll be the last time Julia invites me to her place, I expect." She chuckles and I roll my eyes. My grandmother is fleecing people she's known for years. Great. "So, did Nick show up yet?"

My mood sours. "Yeah, he was here. Had to run back to town to get a part but he'll be back to fix the boiler in a bit."

"That's good." Grams pauses. "Vivian still there with you?"

"No, she hitched a ride back to town with Nick." The thought alone hangs like a dark cloud over my head.

"You let her go?" Grams sounds surprised.

"Yeah, Grams. She has to check on her shop and her daughter." I bite back the smart-ass comment on the tip of my tongue reminding myself I am talking to my grandmother after all. "Would have been nice if you'd have told me about Charlotte and Nick."

"Oh, well, I thought you already knew. I mean, you and Vivian are friends."

"Were friends, Grams. In high school. It's been a while."

"So you're not friends now?" Grams presses.

I sigh and put the eggs on a plate. "It's complicated."

"It's only as complicated as you make it, Andrew." Grams shuffles fabric or something on the other end. "Were you two going at it last night or not?"

"Grams!" Even hearing my grandmother mention a euphemism for sex has my stomach turning.

"Well, were you?"

"I'm not dignifying that with an answer."

"That's an admission if I ever heard one." Grams clears her throat. "You both are obviously invested in this whole thing. What's the problem then?"

"She has her life here, Grams. I can't ask her to give that up and move to Brooklyn."

"And you're not willing to give up your nice fancy office job for the woman you love. Am I right?" She sighs and tuts dramatically. "Youth is wasted on the young."

"I haven't decided what I'm going to do yet. I need to think."

"Fine." Grams agrees. "You do that. We're going to have the festival tonight instead. The roads should be clear."

"Okay, I'll see you tonight."

"Love you."

"Love you too, Grams." I end the call and set the phone aside to finish charging.

As I pour a cup of coffee, I'm left wondering what the hell just happened. Was I caught in some strange continuum where all my life's choices are called into question? I sit down at the table and break the yolks with my fork.

A week ago, I was a successful bachelor with a solid job and financial stability. Now, that part of me feels like a far-off dream. What happened between Vivian and I consumes my thoughts and leaves me wondering what the fuck I should do now because I can't lose her. Not again.

CHAPTER TWELVE

VIVIAN

The snow covers everything, coating tree branches and leaving a white blanket over the forest and fields. The roads are slick but easier to navigate thanks to the plow truck that passed us.

Nick hasn't said anything since we left Ruth's cabin. I don't volunteer any information either. It seems like I don't need to, judging by the look on his face. His brow furrowed, lips locked in a frown. It's like Andrew's sitting in the truck with us causing a weighted tension to pull tighter with every passing moment.

"Did you fuck him?" Nick finally shatters the tension with a sledgehammer.

"Not that it's any of your business, but yes, I did." I glare at him.

Nick's grip on the steering wheel tightens. "He's back in town for one day and you jump his bones."

"Damn it, Nick." I fold my arms across my chest. "Don't you dare start this shit. In case you forgot, we're divorced. Have been for five years."

"Doesn't mean I don't care about you." Nick downshifts and slows as we round a curve. "I don't think you should be throwing yourself at him like that. He's not gonna stick around, you know."

"Listen, I didn't lecture you when you jumped into bed with Anita after our divorce was finalized." I focus on the road as my anger bubbles to the surface. "She didn't stick around either, if I remember correctly."

"You can't leave. What about Charlotte?" he growls. "I still have partial custody. You can't take her away from me."

I pinch my eyes closed. "I have no intention of taking our daughter away from you, Nick. Don't be an asshole."

"I'm being realistic."

"No, you're not. You're being an asshole."

"I still care about you, Vivian. I don't want you to get hurt," he snaps.

My conscience faulters at his confession. "Damn it, Nick. I care about you too, but I'm not in love with you. I've told you this before."

"You can't jump into a relationship with a guy you haven't seen in twenty years and expect it to work out. This isn't a fairy tale."

"Nick, this isn't about Andrew and me. This is about facing the truth. You don't want to let me go, but you have to."

"He hurt you before, Vivian. Making a fool out of you in front of everyone and then running away without a word." Nick's expression softens and he glances at me before making the turn into town. "I won't let him do it again."

"Neither will I, Nick." I smile. "I'm a lot smarter than I was then. Give me some credit."

"I do. That's what scares me." The truck rolls to a stop in front of Buck Wild Beans. "I'll send Charlotte over around five. She's making pies with my mom today."

"That's fine. Thank you for the ride home. I appreciate it." I unbuckle my seatbelt and slide from the cab.

"No problem. And hey," he pauses waiting until our eyes meet. "Just be careful."

"See you later, Nick." I close the door and make my way through the drift to the freshly shoveled sidewalk in front of the coffee shop.

The door's open, and I'm glad Susan had the morning shift today.

"Hey, boss, I was worried about you." Susan calls across the shop. "You're normally here by noon. It's almost one."

"Sorry, I got snowed in up on the mountain."

"It's okay. Guess that storm really pulled a fast one on us. They moved the festival to tonight."

"Oh, that's good. I'm glad all that planning isn't going to go to waste." I motion to the hallway door. "I'm gonna take a shower and change before I take over, that okay?"

"Fine with me. Take your time." Susan waves me off and takes a tray of drinks to the corner table where Merle and Betty are waiting.

I wave to them and slip through the back door that leads upstairs to my apartment over the shop. The whole building is mine, which works to my benefit, but I also never seem able to turn it off. I'm always in the shop, whether I'm on the clock or not.

Inside my space again, I plug my phone in and head right for the bathroom. A hot shower soothes my sore muscles and the ache in my back from sleeping on the floor. Or it could have been from the way Andrew possessed every inch of me last night.

The water sluices over my skin. There are tiny bruises forming on my hips from his fingers. My face heats. I don't remember sex being as invigorating and spontaneous as it was last night. Not that I blame my ex for his lack of enthusiasm, but there's no comparing Nick and Andrew. They're in separate leagues completely.

I push away the wicked memory of Andrew and our steamy night together and wash my hair. When I finally feel clean and refreshed, I turn off the shower and dry off before putting my robe on. Scrunching my hair, I cross into the bedroom to change.

Within twenty minutes, I'm dressed, refreshed, and ready to take on the world. I purposely ignore the guilt churning in the pit of my stomach. *Andrew.* We need to talk.

Tonight. After the festival. Yes. We'll talk. I don't know what the hell I'm going to say to him, but we're adults, it's not like we can't figure out a way to make this work. Right?

A knock at the door startles me. I grab my phone and unlock the door.

"Hello, Vivian, Susan told me I'd find you up here." Ruth stands on my doorstep wearing her ugly Christmas sweater from the night before. The white curls and wrinkled skin show her age, but those sparkling eyes, so much like Andrew's, hold a vitality I envy. "May I come in for a moment?"

"Of course, Ruth. You're always welcome here." I step aside and allow her in. "Would you like something to drink?"

"Oh, no, dear. I'm fine. Thank you." She sits on the small love seat near the far window.

"Is something wrong, Ruth?" I take a seat on the chair across from her.

She waves her hand. "Oh, no. Nothing's wrong." Her gaze studies me. I get the distinct impression I'm being weighed and measured before judgement is rendered.

I shift in my chair. "Good."

"You're in love with him."

I blink twice before I can register her words. "What? Who?"

"My grandson." She wags a finger. "I know he fancied you years ago. Found his notebook laying open on the table once. Had your name scrawled all over the inside of it." Ruth grins. "Had it bad, he did."

My face heats. Did Andrew really do that? I clear my throat. "But it doesn't mean I love him, Ruth. That means he had a crush on me years ago."

Ruth taps the side of her nose with her finger. "You loved him. Always followed him around when you were kids."

"Again, that was twenty years ago, I hardly think it means..."

"You had sex with him last night, didn't you?"

I bury my red-hot face in my hands. "Oh, God."

"God's got nothing to do with this, Vivian." Her eyes sparkle.

"Did he tell you?" I choke out the question through my embarrassment.

"He didn't have to, dear." She winks.

I hide my face again.

"There's nothing to be ashamed of. You're both consenting adults. And sex is the most natural thing in the world." She narrows her gaze a fraction. "Some of my peers think it's better to hide their sexual nature in shame. Fools." Her gaze softens and she takes my hand in hers. "I'm glad you're embracing your desires, dear."

"Ruth, I'm not going to lie. This is awkward."

She pats my hand. "I know, dear. The truth always is."

"Truth?"

"Yes. You and Andrew have been smitten with each other for years. And judging from the sparks I saw yesterday, that time apart did nothing but add more kindling to the fire."

A thought forms in my mind and I can't ignore it. I've long since realized there are no coincidences, and everything happens for a reason. Instead of brushing off the insane thought, I dare to ask the question.

"Did you invite Andrew home to set us up?"

Ruth pulls her hand away and presses it to her chest. "What? That's ridiculous. I asked him home so I could see him. That boy hasn't visited me since he left. I always have to visit him. Rotten child." A grin tugs at the corners of her mouth. "Although, I hoped he would see you and realize what a fool he'd been staying away all these years."

Suspicion confirmed. Ruth is one crafty and wise old woman. "I see. So, no matchmaking on your part then?"

She shrugs. "Maybe a smidgen."

"Mmhmm." I chuckle at her tenacity. "Well, you succeeded with your first stage. But I don't think you considered the long-term complications."

"Complications?" Ruth parrots and cocks her head.

"Andrew isn't going to give up his job in New York to move here, and I can't give up my shop, not to mention relocate Charlotte before her freshman year. Plus, Nick would never let me take his daughter that far away. It'd break his heart." I sigh. "I don't see how it'll work long term, no matter how much chemistry we have or how much I love him."

"You love him." Ruth grins. "That's the first step. The rest will work out, somehow."

"I wish I shared your optimism." I shrug and lean back against the chair.

"The course of true love never did run smooth," Ruth quotes with a solemn tone that strangely resembles a Jedi master. Considering the baby Yoda on her shirt, I should find it comical, but it's more endearing than anything else and I'm comforted by it more than I thought I would be.

"I know."

"Just promise me one thing, Vivian." Ruth slowly rises to her feet. "Talk to Andrew tonight. Tell him what you told me. You're both smart. You'll figure out a solution." She opens her arms wide.

I hug her, holding her close like I held my grandma when she was still around. "Thank you."

"I love you, Vivian. And that daughter of yours. You both keep me young." She pulls back and winks.

"We love you too, Ruth."

I follow her down to the shop and offer a cappuccino, which she accepts with bright-eyed glee. Once I settle into my shift, I pause behind the espresso machine and whisper a little prayer.

A Christmas Eve wish sent straight to heaven. I only hope He sees how much I want this.

CHAPTER THIRTEEN

ANDREW

After Nick returned and ensured the boiler worked efficiently, I cleaned up the cabin, erasing all evidence of the passionate night Vivian and I spent together. I even made sure to wash the blankets.

The afternoon passed quickly between cleaning, showering, and doing laundry. By the time five o'clock rolled around, a flurry of text messages blows up my phone. All from Grams telling me to hurry and the party is starting without me.

I roll my eyes. She's worse than a teenager sometimes. And who the hell taught her to text using emojis? I shove my phone in my pocket and grab my coat before heading out to start my car. It takes ten minutes to clean the damn snow off it.

As much as I loathe Nick's attachment to Vivian, he seemed sincere in his offer to give me a ride into town earlier, which I declined. Instead, he used the plow on the front of his truck to clean out Grams' driveway and wished me luck getting down the mountain in my *fancy* car.

I slide into the driver's seat and groan with bliss at the warmth radiating from the heated leather seats. Yeah, fancy car. Totally fucking worth it. With a bit of maneuvering, I'm able to get turned around and out onto the main road with little trouble. I take it slow down the mountain, aware of the icy curves and deep snowdrifts.

Once I'm on the main road into town, I breathe easier. The roads are clear and salted, which will do a number to my undercarriage, but I'd take that over ending up in a ditch or wrapped around a tree. The sun's already set and the Christmas decorations glow from the streetlamps lining the main street.

Funny, the Christmas decorations don't bother me today nearly as much as they did yesterday. Maybe I'm desensitized to them now because of Grams' overindulgence. I pull into the parking lot across from Buck Wild Beans and the community center where everyone is gathering.

Families wander down the street. Children running ahead throwing snowballs at each other. I can hear the faint strains of Christmas carols coming from the center. It's disgustingly domestic and quaint. I'm surprised I don't gag.

Then I see Vivian through the window of the coffee shop. She's backlit from the lights inside and framed by the sparkling lights in the front window. My heart stops. She's fucking gorgeous. I watch until she disappears and lean my head back against the seat.

What the hell am I doing? I can't let her go. I'd be insane if I did.

I tap on my phone sitting in the holder on the center console and open the recent numbers. I hit the third one and switch the audio to the phone instead of the speaker before dialing.

Third ring and the phone connects.

"Hello."

"Hey, Ben, I hope I'm not interrupting your Christmas party." I tap my fingers on the steering wheel, anxiety churning in my gut threatening to make me sick.

"Nope. Penelope and Evan here helping get the place set up. You change your mind on coming?"

"No. I'm still in Pennsylvania." The lights go out in the coffee shop.

"Oh. Everything okay?"

It's weird to hear Ben talk like this. He's normally much more brusque. "Yeah, everything's fine. You?"

"Of course." He pauses then it comes. "Something you need, or can I get back to helping my wife in the kitchen?"

"Sorry. I'm not sure how to say this, but I need your advice."

Silence fills the line. "Do you need me to call a lawyer?"

I rake my hand through my hair and groan when Vivian steps out of the coffee shop wearing a red wool jacket. My gaze follows her as she heads toward the community center and walks in the side door.

"No, nothing like that." I exhale a breath and spit it out. "I ran into a girl I've loved since high school and I want to make it work with her, but I don't know how."

Silence stretches again until I hear muffled voices on the other end.

"Andrew, are you asking Ben for love advice?" Evan's voice comes on the line.

I pinch my eyes closed and curse my life. Both bosses on the line, fanfuckingtastic. "Hi, Evan. And no, I wasn't asking for advice really. I was explaining the circumstances..."

"That was fast. You left the city yesterday. You say you've loved this girl since high school." Evan whistles low. "That's impressive as fuck, dude."

"Will you let him talk?" Ben interjects.

"What are you guys talking about?" a feminine voice echoes in the background.

"Andrew, our financial guy at Solus, went home for Christmas and he's gotten himself all tied up over a girl he loved since high school."

"Oh my God! That's so sweet!" Her squeal practically shatters my eardrums. "I'm so happy for you, Andrew!"

Wow. I have no words. This is not how I saw this conversation playing out in my head.

"Will you both stop and let him talk, geezus," Ben snaps bringing the other two into submission. "Go ahead, Andrew."

"I'd like to hand in my resignation."

"*What!*" Ben, Evan, and Penelope all shout into the other end of the phone at the same time. Their chatter overlaps as the shock of my words hits them.

The dread I felt upon initiating this call fades away. Peace settles in my chest at my decision. I clear my throat and call their names. Silence slowly settles over the line.

"I know this is sudden, but I've already thought long and

hard about it. I have spoken." I take a breath. "This is the way."

"This is the way," Ben echoes into the phone.

"Fucking nerds," Evan mutters. "Are you sure, Andrew? I mean you don't have to jump into this so quickly. We can..."

"No, this is what I need to do. I've wasted too much time already." My gaze rests longingly at the community center where I know she's waiting. "I love her, and I'm not letting her get away this time."

Penelope's squeal echoes in the phone once more and smile. "We're happy for you. She's a lucky woman."

"Thanks, Penelope."

"Okay, Andrew, if your mind's made up, I won't fight it. We'll finalize details once you get back to the city. It'll be a huge loss to the company, but you deserve happiness." Ben's steady voice reinforces my decision. "Best of luck to you."

"Thank you all."

"Merry Christmas, Andrew." Penelope adds. "Now, go get her."

"I will." The call disconnects and I'm left in the car alone wondering what the hell I just did. Did I really hand in my notice? Holy shit. What am I going to do now? Somehow it doesn't matter, what does matter is seeing Vivian. I need her like I need my next breath. Twenty years. Poof. Gone. No. From now on, it's not about the money or the prestige. It's about her and Charlotte and making sure they have what they need to be happy and whole.

Halfway across the parking lot, my confidence falters. Guilt washes over me. Maybe I should have discussed this with Vivian before I made such a huge decision. I shake my head. Nothing I can do about it now. I square my shoulders and cross the street.

The music grows louder with every step. I'm almost to the door when I collide with a young woman who seems as preoccupied as I am. The impact nearly knocks me into a snowbank.

I reach out and steady her before she tumbles back into the snow-covered hedgerow. "Are you okay?"

She tucks her phone into her pocket and brushes her long

brown hair away from her face. I freeze thinking I've been caught in a time warp and whisked back to my senior year of high school. *Vivian,* I think for half a second until I realize this is her daughter. It has to be.

"Yeah, I'm fine. Sorry, I wasn't watching where I was going. I'm running late, and my mom's gonna kill me." She tucks a long strand of her hair behind her ear and smiles. Shit, she looks so much like Viv did when we were younger.

"You must be Charlotte." I let her go.

Her eyes widen. "How'd you know my name? Who are you?"

"I'm an old friend of your mom's." I offer my hand. "Andrew. It's nice to finally meet you."

She shakes my hand but eyes me with suspicion. "How do you know Mom?"

"We went to high school together. She was my sister's best friend growing up."

"She's never mentioned you." Her hand slips away from mine.

"I've been gone a while." I can't blame her suspicion. If it were my mom, I'd be wary too. Smart kid. "Shall we find her together?"

Charlotte shrugs. "Sure."

I follow her inside the community center. The inside is ten times worse than my grandmother's house. It looks like a Christmas bomb exploded. The scent of hot chocolate and peppermint and cinnamon hangs in the air. We weave through the crowd and the decorations. My gaze shifts through the people, searching for a glimpse of a familiar face.

We walk past Grams, who reaches out and grabs my sweater. I stop and she pulls me close enough she can whisper in my ear. "She's over by the punch. Go get her!" Grams winks as she releases me.

I stumble back stunned and shake my head. Is everyone in on this?

In the far corner, I catch sight of Charlotte. She turns and points in my direction. Behind her is Vivian, who's serving punch. I wave.

She waves.

My heart's pounding in my chest. What if she tells me to fuck off? I pinch my eyes close and silence my inner critic. Steeling myself, I head across the room to where they're waiting for me.

Here goes nothing.

CHAPTER FOURTEEN

VIVIAN

"Mom! There's some guy looking for you." Charlotte startles me when she appears by the punch table, her eyes wide and sparkling with curiosity. "He's cute too."

"Charlotte!" I scowl at her, but my gaze follows her finger as she points toward the man beside Ruth and her poker buddies. *Andrew.* He looks right at us and waves. "Oh."

"Oh?" Charlotte arches a brow. "Mom, is he the reason you never came home last night?"

I wave back at him. *No. Yes. Shit.*

"Why don't you get something to eat?" I smooth my hands over my jeans.

"I ate at Grandma's." Charlotte grins while she watches the play between Andrew and I as he crosses the room.

He looks like he's going to devour me whole. I swallow and grab Charlotte's hand. "Please, go find your friends. Give me a minute, please."

Charlotte chuckles. "Okay, Mom. But only a minute. Looks like you two might need a chaperone."

I frown at her. "Go. I'll find you in a bit."

"Fine." She rolls her eyes when Andrew reaches the table.

"Hey again." He smiles at my daughter.

"Hey." Her grin widens. "I'm gonna go. Have fun. Don't do anything I wouldn't do." She slips away before I can reach out and shake some sense into her.

Andrew chuckles before he turns to face me. His dark hair brushes over his forehead, those mesmerizing eyes lock with mine and I'm transported to the night before when I was wrapped in his embrace and couldn't tell where either one of us began or ended.

"I would've called, but I don't have your number." He shrugs.

I cringe. That makes sense. "I guess we were a little distracted, huh?"

"A little." He offers his hand. "Wanna dance?"

I nod and abandon my post dipping punch. Everyone's occupied at the moment, I can take a break. My hand fits perfectly in his and he leads me onto the dance floor.

His hand rests on my hip and my body warms instantly. I rest my head against his chest as we sway to the music. A slow Christmas jingle I've heard a million times, but I can never remember the name. His grip tightens as he pulls me against him.

"I missed you," he murmurs.

I glance up at him. "Me too."

"Can we talk somewhere?" He seems pale and uncertain. Not the confident man I saw last night.

"Sure." I take his hand and lead him through the community center kitchen and out the back door. We weave around the dumpsters and I quickly unlock the back door of the coffee shop. Inside, I flip the light on in the hallway and gesture to the shop. "Want a coffee?"

"Sure." He follows me as I step behind the counter.

I turn on the machine, and he runs his hand over the steel canister that holds the beans.

"That's quite a machine."

"Yeah, don't ask how much this puppy cost." I laugh and prepare the beans. "Latte, cappuccino, espresso?"

"Double espresso, please."

"Coming right up." I lock the beans into place and hit brew. His arms wrap around me, his cheek beside mine, watching me work.

"This looks complicated." His whisper sends shivers down to my toes. I arch back against him in response.

"It's not." I watch the coffee stream out, the steam and scent wrapping around my head. But I'm distracted by the man holding me tightly against him. "I can teach you."

"Might have to." He kisses my earlobe. "I'm looking for a new job. Got any openings?"

It takes a moment for the words to cut through the lusty haze he's created with his touch and his sexy voice. "Wait, what did you just say?" I spin in his arms and face him. "Seriously, what?"

Andrew's hands rest against the counter behind me. His gaze skims over my face and down to my lips before he sighs. "I'm staying, Viv. If you want me, I'm yours."

Emotion rushes me, wave after wave. Disbelief, joy, uncertainty, and love. Love for this man before me. I cup his face in my hands. "You quit your job? For me?" My voice cracks.

He nods. "I've already talked to my bosses. It's done."

"Why would you do that?" I drop my hands to his chest and give him a shove. "You had an amazing job. Why would you throw it all away for me?"

Andrew grabs my wrists and holds them against his chest. His heart beats steady beneath my hands. "Because I love you, Vivian. I've wasted enough time chasing success. I want happiness. And I want it with you."

Tears burn my eyes and slip down my cheeks. "Andrew." I choke back a sob. "You idiot."

He chuckles and releases my hands to brush the tears from my cheeks with his fingertips. "Why am I an idiot?"

"I don't know." I shrug. "I mean, how do you know this will work? Last night was amazing. You are amazing. I love you; I do. But we've been apart for so long, what if it doesn't work?"

"Then it doesn't work." He shrugs. "Isn't it worth a chance?"

"Yes, of course it is." I fist my hands in his shirt. "Are you sure this is what you want?"

"I've never been more certain of anything in my whole life." He leans closer and presses a soft kiss against my lips. "What do you say? Can we give it a shot?"

I nod fervently. "Yes. Hell yes." I wrap my arms around his neck and kiss him as though I haven't tasted him in years.

His hand slides along my side and under my sweater. I gasp

at the contact and deepen the kiss even more. He pins me to the bar and palms my breast in his hand. "I love you, Viv."

"I love you too." I gasp when he pinches my nipple. "We should get back to the party." I moan as he nips at my throat.

"What's your hurry?"

"Charlotte will be looking..."

"Mom? Andrew? Are you in here?" Charlotte's voice echoes down the hallway.

Andrew groans and steps away reluctantly. His hands drop to his sides, but I see the flex of his fingers as he regains control of his desire. It makes me grin knowing I affect him so much.

"Yeah, honey. We're in here." I call out, tugging down the hem of my sweater and making sure I don't look like I've been making out with my high school crush behind the counter of my coffee shop.

"There you are!" Charlotte appears on the other side of the counter. "Ruth said she saw you head out the back." Her gaze drifts between the two of us and a slow grin splits her lips. "Did I interrupt something?"

Andrew clears his throat, and I elbow him in the ribs. He groans.

"No. You're fine." I pour his espresso in a mug and hand it to him. "Since you're here, we might as well tell you the news." I glance at Andrew. He gives an encouraging nod. "Andrew and I are dating. I thought you should be the first to know."

"And what about me? Am I chopped liver?" Ruth shouts from the illuminated hallway.

"No, Grams. We were going to tell you next." Andrew shakes his head.

I clap a hand over my mouth as the laughter bubbles up.

Ruth comes to stand next to Charlotte on the other side of the counter. They both lean against the polished wooden surface and study us.

"Welcome to the family, kiddo." Ruth nudges Charlotte.

"You were already part of the family, Grandma Ruth." Charlotte hugs her.

"Yes, but now it's official." Ruth winks.

"Wait, I didn't ask her to marry me. We're dating." Andrew slides his arm protectively around my waist.

Ruth scoffs. "It's only a matter of time."

"You sound confident in your assertion, Ruth." I narrow my gaze and grin. "Almost as though you had something to do with this whole thing from the very beginning."

She sniffs. "I don't know what you're talking about. I wanted everyone home for Christmas, that's all."

"Sure, Grams. I know a set up when I see one. You had your hands on this from the moment you called and told me to come home for Christmas." Andrew laughs.

"Whatever is between you two started years before I ever got involved." Ruth hugs Charlotte tighter. "Everyone deserves a chance to fix their mistakes."

I turn and face Andrew. "Was I a mistake?"

"That feels like a trick question." He thinks for a moment before continuing. "Yes and no."

"Not an answer." I poke his side.

He laughs. "Fine. I don't regret kissing you at the Christmas dance senior year, but I do regret pushing you away and not punching those assholes in the face when they made fun of you. Leaving without making things right, that was my biggest mistake."

My heart aches with joy at his words. "Guess we'll have to make up for it now. Won't we?"

Andrew hugs me against his chest. "Yes, we will."

Charlotte does a little dance with Ruth and we all laugh.

Strains of the Imperial March fills the air. We all freeze wondering where the music is coming from.

Andrew reaches into his pocket and pulls out his phone. "Hello?"

We stare at him in curiosity.

"Yeah. No, I understand." His jaw drops open and closes again before he meets my gaze. "Yes, absolutely. Thank you, sir. Ben. I appreciate it. Merry Christmas." He hangs up the phone and stares at it for a second before laughter overtakes him.

"What?" I tug at his sleeve. "Who was that?"

"My boss, Ben. He told me I'm not allowed to quit. He's willing to let me telecommute for as long as I need." Andrew grabs me by the waist and swings me around. "I can stay, *and* I can keep my job."

Elation consumes me. "I'm so happy for you, Andrew." I throw my arms around his neck and kiss him. "What a wonderful gift."

"Yeah, it is." His gaze meets mine and the heat simmers between us.

"Come on, Charlotte. These two need some alone time." Ruth links arms with Charlotte and heads for the back door. "Have fun, lovebirds!"

"I love you, Viv." Andrew's voice is breathy and full of promise.

"Ditto." I grin. "Merry Christmas."

"Merry Christmas, sweetheart."

I wrap my hand around his and pull. "Come on. Let's go upstairs, we can celebrate properly."

"Whatever you say. I'm all yours."

I wink at him over my shoulder. "Damn straight. Now, let's make up for lost time, shall we?"

And they shared the naughtiest Christmas ever…
Merry Christmas.

The End

CRAVING MORE?

READ ON FOR A TEASER FOR

A LOCKDOWN LOVE AFFAIR

&

A HOLIDAY LOVE AFFAIR

A LOCKDOWN LOVE AFFAIR

CHAPTER ONE
LOCKDOWN

BEN

LOCKDOWN DAY 1

Don't panic. It's not the end of the world. It only feels like it.

I grip the remote tighter instead of throwing it against the wall. I want to see it shatter, but the thought of cleaning up another mess leaves me desperate for some form of control. Damn it. I have plans. I have work to do. If they lock the city down, I'm done. I groan when the mayor steps up to the microphone and announces the fate of the city, at least for the foreseeable future.

Non-essential businesses are closed until further notice. City-wide lockdown. Stay at home. Self-quarantine.

The words hover in the air like a poisonous cloud threatening to choke me.

Damn it. I shoot to my feet and, this time, throw the remote. The satisfaction of impact is short-lived. Just like I knew it would be, and now I have to buy a new remote. One more fucking thing. Great. Just wonderful. I stalk to the TV and jerk the plug out of the wall. Unnecessary, yes. But it makes me feel better.

My phone pings in rapid succession as a flurry of texts come in. I rub my hands over my face. Why? Of all the times for a pandemic to hit, why now? Why couldn't it have hit after the merger? Now I'm stuck in my goddamn apartment, and I sure as hell can't finalize this deal from home. What if I need files from the office? Specific records? The things I need to do my job might as well be half a world away. We are so fucked.

I stare out the window at the Brooklyn skyline. The sun casts long shadows over the city as it sets. I catch a glimpse of the neighboring building whose rooftop is nearly level with my floor. Dying sunlight highlights the pots and raised garden beds occupying part of the roof. The small table and two chairs sit empty. I rack my brain. Were those there last week?

I shake my head. It doesn't matter. Normally, I'm not home to even notice anything outside my windows. This apartment is merely a place to crash when I'm not at the office.

My phone pings again. I have to deal with it sooner or later. The company needs direction, and with Evan out of town I need to be on my game. Lockdown or not, I'm still in charge. There're mountains of work to do until the merger is complete. I can't take the chance of anything going wrong.

I grab the phone. Fourteen messages. Half of them are from Evan. If I don't call him, he'll keep blowing up my phone. I hit the call button.

"Holy shit, you returned my call. Are you dying?" Evan sounds surprised.

"What do you want?" I pointedly ignore his snarky question.

"I saw the news." The unspoken implications pull tight like a rubber band.

I want to snap, but I grind my teeth instead. "I have it under control."

"I know. I'm not worried about the merger. I'm worried about you."

"Why?"

"Because you live at the office, Ben. Do you even have food at your apartment?"

My gaze drifts to the kitchen. Do I have anything here?

"This is Brooklyn. I can get a pizza delivered at 3:00 am if I want it."

Evan grumbles under his breath. "Dickhead."

"You know I can hear you." I open my laptop and press a few keys, pulling up my inbox.

"Well, you are. Anyway, are you going to be okay working from home for a few days?"

"Yeah, I have some of the files here. Once things relax a little, I'll get back in the office and finalize the paperwork for Mr. Kennedy."

"I'll try to get back to the city as soon as I can."

"Why? There's nothing for you to do here but sit on your ass." I pause for effect. "Wait, you do that normally."

"You're a riot. No wonder you're still single."

"So are you. Or did you find the new love of your life in the Poconos?" I'm sick of lectures on my inability to connect with a woman from someone who finds his soulmate every time he travels.

"No." The waver in his voice betrays him.

"Bullshit."

"Fine. There might be someone, but it's nothing serious."

"Keep telling yourself that." I scan the inbox and find an email from Empire Industries. "Has Mr. Kennedy reached out to you since you left?"

"No. Why?"

I read the email aloud, and my heart sinks. Shit.

"He wants the financials on top of the proposals?" Evan whistles low. "Do you have access to that stuff from home?"

"Not all of it." Panic claws at the back of my throat. I force it down. "But that shouldn't matter."

"Do you need me to come back to the city?" Evan's reliable, but when it comes to this kind of stuff, he's more trouble than help.

"No, I've got it under control." I take a deep breath. "What day are you coming back?"

"Sunday night."

"Okay. Go enjoy your trip. I've got work to do."

"Don't overthink it, Ben."

I scoff. "Later."

Once I disconnect the call, I toss the phone aside and rake my hand through my hair.

"Shit." I glance at the pack of cigarettes sitting near the door by my keys. I'm dying for one. I've been trying to quit for weeks. This is a hell of a time to give them up.

I settle for a beer from the fridge, ignoring the absence of any real food in the refrigerator, and collapse on the couch. I scroll through the rest of the unread emails.

There is plenty of work to keep me busy. Just because I'm at home and not at the office doesn't mean I can't be productive. Besides, the lockdown can't last that long. This city has seen some shit. It's been through terrorist attacks and financial recessions. And if the past is anything to go by, New Yorkers are resilient and badass. There's no way a city of this size and fortitude will come to a screeching halt because of a global pandemic.

Even as I think it, dread settles like a dark cloud over my head.

PENELOPE

LOCKDOWN DAY 1

I set the last few items in the box and close the lid. There. That should do it. I nod approvingly at the stack of boxes littering the hallway. Finally. It took me four months to sort through all of my grandparents' possessions. After they both passed away in November, I found every excuse to avoid going through their belongings. It hurt too much every time I opened a door, only to find the room filled with empty reminders. They meant everything to me, and now they're gone.

Sadness settles around me for a moment. "I miss you both so much." My hand slides over the box. As the eldest granddaughter, I had the strongest bond with them. Nearly every summer and holiday meant a trip to the city to stay with Grandma and Grandpa. So many memories lay within this historic brownstone. I cried when the lawyer told me I'd inherited it. I'd never thought I'd find myself living in Brooklyn, especially in a world without my grandparents. When I moved in, the small reminders of them became overwhelming. After a few months, I found it easier to deal with their estate than to drown in it. It helped me process the overwhelming loss. Still, I miss them desperately, but at least they're together and at peace.

A week before my trip to visit them for Thanksgiving, they died in a horrible car accident. I should have been here, but I wasn't. Nothing can change that ache in my heart telling me I could have done something to prevent it.

No, I will not dwell on it. Not today. I can't change the past with regrets and wishful thinking. I glance around the house and see how much I've accomplished. It needed to be done. So I did it, for them and for me.

Now, if I could just find the motivation to haul this stuff to the empty basement apartment Grandpa used for storage.

I grab my keys and open the front door. It'll take a few trips, but I think I can manage it tonight.

Ooof. I collide with someone on my front doorstep. "Oh, my goodness, I'm so sorry." I straighten quickly.

"Quite alright, Miss Weiss." My grandparents' neighbor, Mr. Donovan, smiles at me before offering a piece of paper. He's in his sixties and normally looks quite spry. Today, exhaustion lines his face. "I take it you've seen the news?"

I stare at him puzzled. "What news?"

His gray brows furrow. "The mayor just announced a city-wide lockdown."

I blink at him, confused. "Lockdown?"

"Yes. You cannot leave your home unless it's for a medical emergency or to purchase necessary supplies. All non-essential businesses are required to close." His eyes widen behind his bifocals. "I've never seen anything like it in all my years."

"Wow." I glance at the paper in my hand. A notice from the city with instructions and contact information. "Thank you."

"Where are you going?"

"I have to take some things to the basement and then run to the market for dinner." I gasp. "Am I still allowed to do that?"

"It should be fine." He nods. "But tomorrow, I would advise staying home if you can. This virus is nothing to sneeze at." He chuckles at his own pun.

"Am I able to tend my garden on the roof at least?" I ask, tucking the paper into my pocket.

He nods after a moment of thought. "I don't see a problem with that. It's your roof. Not like you're wandering around the city aimlessly." He winks. "I'm looking forward to some of those fresh herbs and vegetables you promised me."

"Of course." A wave of relief washes over me. At least I have my garden. "They've already started sprouting. It's sure to be a bountiful harvest."

He smiles. "I hope so. If you need anything, please, don't hesitate to call me."

"I will." I wave as he walks down the steps. "Thank you."

Over the next hour, I transfer the boxes from the house upstairs to the basement apartment. Grandpa had converted the basement of the brownstone into a separate apartment in the hope I would come live in the city permanently. I wish I had taken him up on the offer after I graduated college. Regrets only serve as a hurdle, and I am determined to move forward. When I finally collapse on the couch, it's completely dark outside.

Damn. I wanted to check on the garden. It will have to wait until morning. I shower and run to the corner market to pick up some items for dinner as well as supplies for the week. Once I'm back home, I make some dinner before flopping in front of the television. I ignore cable completely and turn on Netflix. They just released the new season of the science fiction show I love.

After my grandparents' accident, I moved to the city to execute their will. Their estate covers my expenses, so there's no rush to find a job. Not that I've thought about it until now. Am I even going to stay in the city? It's not like I have anything keeping me here. Still, it would be an adventure, living the city life after growing up in rural Pennsylvania. Maybe I'll take some time and see what Brooklyn has to offer me.

Even if the city wasn't on lockdown, I would have never noticed. The market was busier than usual, but that tended to happen in the evenings. It took me a few months to acclimate to life in the city. I may never get used to the hustle of city living, although it is exciting.

I have a gorgeous home, a promising rooftop garden, and financial stability. What more could a girl possibly ask for?

I settle on the couch and snuggle beneath my favorite afghan. The show starts, and I'm drawn into the new season. I wish Lucy were here to watch it with me. I reach for the phone to call her and hang up when she doesn't answer. Damn, she must be working second shift at the hospital this week.

Then I remember the lockdown and the pandemic. I hope she's okay. I make a mental note to call her in the morning and then lose myself in the show.

A LOCKDOWN LOVE AFFAIR

(BEN AND PENELOPE'S STORY)

AVAILABLE NOW

A Holiday Love Affair

Chapter One
The Imaginary Evan

Lucy

October

Today my best friend will marry the man who stole her heart. Fortunately, their wedding will be a simple, uncomplicated affair. Two people, madly in love, with a handful of witnesses and a judge. Over and done in five minutes. Wham, bam, where's the afterparty?

Just like every single one of my relationships.

I wish I could say I love weddings. But I don't. I hate them. Almost as much as I hate holidays. The horrified looks on my friends' faces when I tell them solidifies my distaste.

The underwire of the strapless bra digs into my side and I shift uncomfortably. "Penelope, are you done? Seriously, the car's out front waiting for us."

"Coming!" Penelope's voice echoes down the hallway.

I shift from one foot to the other. These heels are killing me. I'd give anything for my Danskins right now, but I want to look nice for my friend. This is her day. I bite my tongue as the complaint congeals on the tip of it.

Penelope appears in the living room doorway wearing a cream-colored, pin-up style gown with lace trim that accents her dark hair and wide, hopeful eyes. Not a traditional gown by any standard, but it suits her perfectly. She smooths her hand over the loose French braid and along the pearl choker at her throat.

"Do I look okay?" The flutter in her voice betrays her nerves.

"You're fucking gorgeous." I take her hand in mine and squeeze it. "Now, let's go, or Ben will call Joey to send out a search party."

Her brilliant smile eases the twisting anxiety in my gut. "Thanks for being here with me. I know how much you hate this stuff."

"You're lucky I love you so much." I grin. "Besides, I'm only in this for dinner afterward. Ben did get us reservations at The River Cafe."

"You're ridiculous." Penelope pauses. Her gaze glides over my body. *Here it comes.*

"You look amazing!" She grins and pulls the wool wrap around her shoulders. "I don't think I've ever seen you in a dress before."

"And you probably never will again." I shake my head. "Scrubs are far superior. They let my body breathe!" I pull at the underwire again. "This bra is going to kill me."

"Well, don't take it off until *after* dinner, okay?" Penelope winks and moves toward the door.

"Fine." I stumble, nearly twisting my ankle in these three-inch heels. "Damn it. These things are coming off as soon as I sit my ass down at dinner."

"Deal. It's only going to be the four of us at dinner anyway." Penelope opens the door and the cool October breeze drifts across my skin.

"The infamous Evan will be joining us?" I can't keep the snark from my tone. I've heard Penelope and Ben talk about Evan for months, and yet I've never seen him. Personally, I don't think he exists except as a blurred figure in their imagination.

During the pandemic lockdown and subsequent chaos, I lost myself in work. Six days a week, swing shifts and overtime. Some days I felt dead on my feet. I can only blame myself though. I took every shift they offered me at the hospital, and I didn't stop. I didn't want to. Work keeps me grounded in the midst of all the uncertainty.

Today is the first day I've taken for myself since January, and it's not really for myself. The head nurse practically threw a party when I asked for some time off, even if it was only one day.

"Oh, that's right." Penelope carefully makes her way down the steps of the brownstone. She turns to face me. "You haven't met him yet, have you?"

I shake my head and motion for her to get into the car first. The limo driver nods before closing the door. The leather seats are cool beneath my fingertips. "I still think he's a figment of your imagination."

Penelope laughs. "Just because you haven't met him doesn't mean he's not real."

"If you say so." I inhale deep and eye the mini bar in the center console.

As if reading my mind, Penelope grabs the open bottle of chilled champagne and pours two glasses. "Here. This will take the edge off."

"This is your wedding day, not mine." I accept the glass. "I should be calming your nerves, not the other way around."

"Why would I be nervous?" She laughs and lifts the champagne in a toast. "To us."

"To us." We clink glasses and I down half the shimmering liquid in one swallow. The bubbles tickle my throat. I'm much more of a whisky girl, but the fancy stuff isn't bad.

I'm halfway through my second glass when we pull up in front of the courthouse. I finish the champagne and set the glass aside. "Ready?"

Penelope nods, a huge grin painted on her lips.

When we step from the car, I notice Ben first. His broad shoulders and tall stature make him hard to miss, plus he's handsome as the devil. Penelope's lucky her stalker neighbor was a sexy, eligible bachelor. My heart sinks. Some girls have all the luck.

"Ladies, I was wondering if you'd ever show up." Ben's voice is stern but it echoes with humor. Lucky girl indeed.

"Sorry, I couldn't find my grandma's pearls." Penelope touches the choker at her throat.

"Lucy." Ben acknowledges my presence with a polite nod and a half smile.

"Stalker Ben." I grin at him. "Congratulations."

"Thank you." He turns his head for a brief moment and I follow his gaze.

My heart drops into sinus tachycardia. I press my hand against my sternum and take a deep breath. My mind races. *Calm down. It's a man. It's not like you've never seen one before. Get a grip, girl.*

If Ben were a handsome devil, then this most certainly would be his angelic equivalent. The man smiles and my body bursts into flames. A boyish charm laced with mischief glints in his eyes, but his aura is downright seductive. Boy next door meets sinful fantasy. What the hell? I shake off the unexpected physical reaction and extend my hand.

"Lucy Mackewitz. You must be imaginary Evan." My voice sounds stronger than I feel when I address the man who looks like he stepped out of a *Hugo Boss* advertisement.

He chuckles and grasps my hand in a firm clasp. Damn, he's strong. My gaze rakes over him, from his perfectly kept dirty blond hair, over his broad shoulders, and down to his trim waist. Does he live in the gym? His warmth sinks into me and it takes a tremendous amount self-control not to launch myself at him like a starving beast. *Calm down. This isn't the first time you've been struck by insta-lust. Control your fucking hormones, woman.*

"Evan Waldorf. It's nice to finally meet you, Lucy. Ben and Penelope have told me so much about you." His gleaming smile oozes charm. That crystalline blue gaze holds mine and I swear I see a flash of hunger. Or is it amusement? I shake the thoughts from my mind and force a saccharine smile.

"Of course, they have." I glare at Ben and Penelope who seem riveted at the byplay between me and Evan.

He releases my hand and the immediate pang of loss leaves my brain whiplashed.

"Don't you two have an appointment with the judge in the courtyard?" I ignore the man standing far too close to me and focus on my friend and her soon-to-be husband.

Evan's chuckle makes the hair on my arms prickle with awareness.

As if shaken from a trance, Penelope turns to Ben and pulls his arm. "Come on. Let's get married." He nods and takes her hand. Together they mount the stairs leading to the lovely fountain in front of the historic courthouse.

"Shall we?" Evan's silken baritone wraps around me.

I arch a brow in his direction and note his arm offered in invitation. I can't trust myself to take it. Instead, I pull my coat tighter and follow Penelope and Ben up the stairs.

Evan Waldorf was better left as a blur in my imagination. At least there he wasn't a threat to the vow I'd made years ago, let alone my friendship with Penelope and Ben. *It never ends well.* I remind myself with every step I climb. *Don't encourage him. Just walk away.*

As we approach the judge waiting beside the fountain, I sense Evan's presence and I steel myself a bit more. Damn it, I hate weddings. Is it over yet?

EVAN

OCTOBER

From the moment I saw her, I knew she was the one. Lucy Mackewitz, wrapped in a deep purple coat with her auburn hair tousled and curled, stepped out of the limousine and into my heart.

Outside in the courtyard, the ceremony lasts fifteen minutes. Simple and sweet. Completely appropriate considering Ben hates a big production of anything. He looks at Penelope in a way I've never seen before. Like she's the only person in the world who matters. I'm happy for him. Truly. He deserves it.

Penelope glows with joy as they make their way down the steps. She looks lovely in her vintage ivory lace gown.

I tuck my hands in my pockets and wait for them to climb into the limo. Lucy comes to a stop beside me. I study her profile, the soft curve of her cheek and aquiline nose. Her rosebud lips purse as she shifts her attention to me.

"It's rude to stare." I can't tell if her tone is sarcastic or condescending. Either way, I prefer a challenge.

"Fine. I won't tell you about the smear of lipstick on your cheek."

Her eyes widen a fraction before she leans down and checks her reflection in the limo window. She scoffs and glares at me over her shoulder.

"After you." I stifle a grin and gesture to the open door.

She huffs and joins Ben and Penelope in the car. I chuckle. She's so easy to rile and this knowledge amuses me. I'm kicking myself it took this long to meet her.

I take my seat beside her and across from Ben and Penelope for the ride to the park. She crosses her arms and leans against the far side of the car. Penelope dominates the conversation as she chatters with excitement. Lucy joins in and slowly the tension eases.

My gaze shifts from Lucy to Ben, who's eyeing me with an unreadable expression. Shit. I have to be careful. He's more observant than most people think.

Ben thinks I fall in love every other month. With every new city I visit, a new girl. He's only partially right. It doesn't take much for a woman to capture my attention. I'm a sucker for a pretty face, and I know it. Penelope thinks I'm a hopeless romantic, but the truth is, I'm lonely and I'm not getting younger. The search is fucking exhausting, and it's not getting easier.

Ever since Ben found Penelope, it's like he's realized life doesn't revolve around work. While that bodes well for everyone at the office, I can't help feel like now Ben's hyper aware of my lack of companionship. I glance at him across the limo. He's distracted by his wife. I bite my tongue and smile. If this wasn't my best friend's wedding, I would think this whole evening was a setup.

We stop at Brooklyn Bridge Park and take some photographs with the Brooklyn Bridge and the Manhattan skyline in the background before walking to The River Cafe. We arrive at the restaurant at five thirty, and my stomach grumbles at the thought of the dinner awaiting us.

I offer to escort Lucy into the restaurant like I did at the courthouse. She blatantly ignores me and follows behind the newlywed couple. This woman. I can't explain it, but with every rebuff she burrows deeper beneath my skin.

I rub my hand across my jaw and lag behind. Not that I'm complaining. The view from the rear is as mesmerizing as the rest of her. As if she senses my perusal, she glares at me over her shoulder.

If she were any other woman, I'd sprinkle on a little charm and have her eating from the palm of my hand. But I doubt that will work with Lucy. She's sharp and shrewd. I can't help but wonder if she's fighting whatever this is brewing between us or she truly has no interest in pursuing it.

The romantic lighting and delicate music from a live string quartet floats through the open air outside of the restaurant. The waiter leads us to a garden area outside where the table sits beside a romantic dance floor strung with tiny, sparkling lights. Once we reach our table, I can't help but feel like the third, well, fourth wheel. Ben and Penelope have eyes only for each other, no matter how hard they try to include us in the conversation. Lucy seems equally uncomfortable. She takes a healthy drink of her wine and avoids my gaze.

I glance around noting how empty the restaurant is and wonder if Ben pulled some strings to ensure we'd be the only guests out here tonight. He's such a romantic, even though he'd never admit it.

After we order, Penelope jumps to her feet and pulls Ben

toward the small dance floor. I watch with equal parts horror and amazement because I know Ben has no rhythm whatsoever. Yet I'm stupefied when Ben pulls her into his arms and waltzes her across the floor with ease.

"Well, fuck me."

Lucy chokes on her wine.

I turn in time to see her flushed face disappear behind a large white napkin. She coughs a few times attempting to clear her throat.

"Was it something I said?" I lean a bit closer.

Her green eyes appear over the napkin and narrow as though honing in on my person, ready to deploy a heat-seeking missile. She clears her throat a few more times before setting the napkin aside. Color blooms in her cheeks and I'm left wondering if it's the same color that paints her skin when she climaxes.

A wicked smile curves my lips. Her frown deepens.

I stand and offer my hand. "Let's dance."

"Why?" Skepticism plays across her delicate features.

"Because this is a wedding, and we should be celebrating with our friends." I grab her hand and pull her to her feet.

Lucy fights against my hold for a moment but concedes and follows me to the dance floor. I place my left hand on her hip and take her hand with my right. She's rigid against me and her gaze remains fixed on something in the distance.

"Relax," I murmur, drawing her closer. Her satin gown slides against my suit creating friction and heat. She softens against me a fraction. "I don't bite hard."

She scoffs and tries to pull away. I hold her tight and spin her on the floor.

"Must you make everything a sexual innuendo?"

"I apologize. I wasn't aware I was." Her scent teases me, a sweet touch of coconut and honey. I want to bury myself in her hair and devour her.

We dance in silence for a moment and our surroundings fade into the background.

"We can't do this." Her words are so soft, I barely hear

them.

"Do what?"

"This. Whatever this is."

"Dancing?" I can't help but tease. I know exactly what she's talking about, but I want her to work for this. I want to hear the words from her sinful looking mouth.

"Evan," she growls my name and instantly I'm hard. "Don't make me say it."

"Say what?" I layer extra charm into those two syllables.

"I refuse to ruin my friendship with Penelope and Ben over a fling." Her piercing eyes bore into mine. "That's all it would be. A fling. A one-night stand. Nothing more."

The air around us goes still as the music comes to an end. We stand there staring at each other. I want to kiss her and prove her wrong. We could be so much more. Can't she feel it? This chemistry between us?

"So you feel it too?" I grin. "We can make it work." She fits against me perfectly and I refuse to release her.

"No, Evan. We can't." She pulls away and turns her back to me...to us.

Disappointment and I are old friends, but this time it leaves me off-balance and floundering. The loss is poignant and it settles deep in the pit of my stomach with finality. It was over before it ever had a chance to begin. That knowledge hurts more than nearly losing the business I built from scratch.

We return to the table and pretend everything is fine for Penelope and Ben's sake. They don't need to know. But I can't help but wonder what might have been if she'd only have given me a chance.

A HOLIDAY LOVE AFFAIR

(EVAN AND LUCY'S STORY)

AVAILABLE NOW

OTHER BOOKS BY KIRSTEN S. BLACKETER
CRAVING 1985 SERIES

When I Found You
Can't Fight This Feeling
She Gives Love a Bad Name
Owner of a Lonely Heart
Just What I Needed

HISTORICAL

An Irresistible Shadow
A Shadow's Kiss
Mississippi Moonshine
Deceiving the Earl
Jewel of Winter
At Winter's Demand
Under Winter's Control
Seducing Winter's Gentleman
Stealing the Widow's Heart
Seduction on the Alpine Express
Temptation on the Alpine Express

CONTEMPORARY

A Lockdown Love Affair
A Holiday Love Affair
Mistletoe and Mistakes
Confessions of a Fangirl
Confessions of a Gamer Girl
Confessions of a Glamour Girl
The Flight Before Christmas

FANTASY/FAIRYTALE

Curse of the Huntsman's Jewel
The Huntsman's Revenge

PIRATES AND PERSUASION

Queen Takes Hook

ABOUT THE AUTHOR
KIRSTEN S. BLACKETER

Kirsten S. Blacketer is a multi-published indie author of both historical and contemporary romance. When she's not writing, she homeschools her two children and enjoys time with her family. In those moments of freedom, she devours romance novels while sipping a glass of wine. Age has only shown her that writing villains can be just as fun as heroes. Her next life goals are to write a New York Times Bestseller and one day have Adam Driver play a starring role in a film version of one of her books. A girl can dream, right?

Read more at **http://kirstensblacketer.com.**

ALSO WRITES AS JEN BRADLEE

9 781966 905172